Rob Roensch has published short fiction in *Slice*, *HOBART* and *Epoch*. He lives with his wife and daughters in Baltimore, Maryland and teaches at Towson University.

D1302109

THE WILD FLOWERS OF BALTIMORE

ROB ROENSCH

SALT

CROMER

PUBLISHED BY SALT PUBLISHING
12 Norwich Road, Cromer, Norfolk NR27 0AX United Kingdom

First published by Salt Publishing, 2012

Printed and bound in the United States by Lightning Source Inc.

Typeset in Paperback 9.5/14.5

ISBN 978 1 84471 907 5 paperback

1 3 5 7 9 8 6 4 2

For Carrie and Tully and Penny

CONTENTS

THE DOGS OF BALTIMORE

I do not want to talk about what happened in the spring.
This is the story of the summer: the dog dies.

The dog is a mutt, large-spaniel size, black with graying
whiskers around his nose. He is deaf, and his back legs do
not work, but he never whines. The dog is blind and I have
looked into his eyes. His eyes are not white and blank and
gleaming, like the eyes of a Greek marble bust, nor are
they simply cloudy. His eyes are wormy. Not full of silence
but full of goo. I force myself to look.

I have to wrap him in a towel so he does not pee on
me when I pick him up (surprisingly heavy, because he
does not help) and carry him out into the little backyard
to lay him on the patch of grass so he can feel the sun. I
sit with the dog and touch his head and speak soothing
words: Don't worry dear, that sound is only the man at
the other end of the block with his circular saw. I will then
remember that the dog is deaf. He searches for my face
with his nose.

I am working this summer as a dogwalker. I am out of

college and I do not live here in Baltimore and I am leaving when August is over. My roommates are gone. The two with money are in Europe. The rest of my friends had leases that were up the first of July. I walk dogs all day on hot sidewalks and in the evenings I set a fan on the floor facing me and I order a giant cheese-steak with mayonnaise and watch baseball on ESPN. There is no beer in the refrigerator and I do not much mind. I am more or less alone but I do have the dogs. I prefer their company to mine.

All day, I try not to think about what happened in the spring.

My theory is that the summer will go on forever.

Much of the job is practical—I think about many things while I work, but I also keep a careful eye out for trashcans. The shit has to go somewhere.

I am not a very good dogwalker. The problem is walking dogs is much more than walking dogs. There are parking spots to find, unfamiliar stop signs to roll through blindly. There are litter boxes to scoop and cats to accidentally let escape. There is dog food in one of thirty white cabinets. There are collars to remember to take off when you leave, please, that I forgot to take off and received phone calls about from frantic women whose dogs are the children they never had. There are intercom systems with many buttons to press at frantically while the alarm (keypad on the other side of the kitchen) screams murder.

In certain neighborhoods, everyone is old, even the young. In these neighborhoods, I am watched. People sit on the steps of their brick rowhouses, on park benches, on lawn chairs watering their sidewalks with hoses and watch me. I try not to make eye contact. I act like I am a very busy kid, a busy man, which I am. I'm working. I'm trying to remember this city where I will never live again and I'm trying to figure out why it is important to remember the city, why anything is important at all.

Fireworks: when you see them you see so much, such piercing specific color, such designs intricate as a spider web. But then, later, try to remember one explosion. Try to remember a color.

I see so much more when I work. I used to have work-study at the library, but that wasn't work, that was staring at girls, staring at the computer, staring at the textbook I hadn't opened the whole semester. When I wasn't at the library I was going somewhere other than where I was, to class, to lunch, down to the bar, out to the gym to play ball, to the coffeeshop to cram. Now I am not going anywhere in particular, I am walking around the block until it is time to walk around another block. Everything that I see is the opposite of work, it is the world, it has the quality of a glass of cold water.

The pattern of a maroon tank top and black bra straps and white apron strings around the neck and back of the girl at the coffeeshop, lovely and functional and intricate.

Baltimore is mostly ugly, ill when it is hot and smoggy, but it has a certain rhythm to it that almost makes it not-ugly, which is sad — blocks and blocks of red brick or sort-of-orange brick or formstone (like sandy concrete) rowhouses with the same white marble steps, or with the same patch of front porch, or with the same stained glass above the door. The rhythm of corner bars and churches (too many of both, it seems).

The skyline is unimpressive. There is trash floating in the harbor. And there is always noise — something is being jackhammered apart, something is being nailed to something else.

There is Rust Belt old-empty-factory-rotting-pier decay and new condos with cavernous garages shoehorned in along the old streets. There are aquarium-t-shirt-tourists and yuppies-drinking-wine-in-restaurant-windows and absurd hipsters in their artful little pants and old local burned-tan crazies to scowl at everything.

But the city is beautiful in the early summer evening when the tones of the sunset match the tones of the brick and soften them. The earth and sidewalk radiate out the held heat of the day which is only now, in memory, in ending, finally gentle, human. A pleasant weariness. The idea of the not-all-that-distant green and living bay like a breeze; then an actual breeze. The sense not of lives lived or to be lived but the end of this one day, this one end, the life being lived, the city warm and pale red, leaning calmly into the ordinary night.

The great white lab is pleased to offer me a dry squooshed bird.

I am often asked for directions but I am not very helpful. Even when I know the way I freeze up. After all, I don't live here. Sorry, I say.

Last winter, before what happened, I thought I would maybe be a photographer, but I did not have the money for all that film. A lame excuse. I could also say I did not have the patience, which is not true. I can sit on a bench for hours and watch a dog poke its nose into long grass. What I couldn't abide was the difference between the idea I had and what actually came out. Such as this idea: a girl with long hair and a long neck, I'd have her close her eyes and stand still and I'd tape her hair in streams to the window behind her, light hazing in. It would be strange and funny and sad, a memory warped with a dream. But the thing just looked like a girl with her hair taped to a window. I could not find what I needed in the actual world.

I am trying not to be this way.

Sometimes, people on the street cringe away from my dog in great, absurd fear.

It is the summer of the cicadas, these zzzing incompetent cockroaches. They are not beautiful or interesting or ugly — they do not even sting. They are just everywhere, screaming.

When it rains it rains and I get wet. I smell like the dogs. At least the sidewalks are clearer of foot traffic; at least a breath of water and silence — but I don't romanticize rain more than that. I don't watch the rain or listen to it, I work through it, despite it.

If a bunch of geese is a flock then a bunch of keys is an insanity. Only one is right, and even the one that is right will not work.

I am terrified by the homes of the semi-rich. A great framed Thomas Kincade painting of a country house with candy-colored porch-lights. Inexplicably enormous silver urns. The same subtly expensive water faucet. Art dedicated to the martini. How could anyone find these things beautiful?

There are mountain bikes in dining rooms, spaceship stereos left on to the lite-rock station, to deter lite-rock fearing cat burglars. There are bare rooms with elaborate mirrors. One bookcase with nothing but every single book John Grisham ever wrote, in hardback, next to a breathtaking view of the harbor from a great height.

I often have to go into this luxury apartment building that looks like a mutant shopping mall/middle school — all this textured stone and glass and that sort of weak turquoise against beigy-pink. The elevators are spacious and mirrored and well-ventilated and fast, and the people in them often make conversation with me. Good day for a walk, they say, sunglasses on top of head, bottle of water in hand. I sense that they know the dog with the leather leash is not mine. I am only the Dogwalker. I hate them.

Every now and then, when I watch the evening news,

I will see some ordinary house or city block that I had driven past that morning now cordoned off with police tape and I'll think I was there when it was happening.

The house of the old dog is unique among the houses I enter. There are bookshelves full of books by authors I do not know. The walls are orange, hung with garage-sale art — a terrifying clown, a not unlovely painting of the sea. The rugs intricate and musty, unwashed-out bowls of spaggettios in the sink.

The dog exists on a dog bed in front of their couch. I imagine the owners of the house sitting on that couch, sipping beers, watching a foreign movie on tape, touching the dog with their bare feet, the dog sleeping.

The dog bed is covered with towels. When one is soiled, I put it on the back steps and replace it with another from a stack on the rocking chair. The stack of towels is large, fifteen of them at least. Odd that two people would own so many towels, and so many so bright. That stack of towels — orange and yellow and electric blue, all clean and folded — is the most optimistic and sad thing I have ever seen.

My father says he can get me a job in the shipping department at his work. He says they are always hiring college boys. He says this without anger, without humor, in his new fatalistic way. He even says I can ride to work with him. My mom tells me she saw David from high school in the grocery store in his Coast Guard uniform. She says Mrs. Woods told her that Mandy from high school is going to have a baby.

She doesn't want to talk about what happened either.

Maybe, she says, I should think about applying to law school.

What consolation? Some are not dead. All windows face the sea.

I don't read much but I have been trying. My roommates left some things: a pornstar poster, a box of wild rice, a few nerf footballs, textbooks they were too lazy to sell back. Introduction to Philosophy. Most of it I don't understand, some I already knew. Some didn't seem important. I liked reading about Kierkegaard: living ethically means not that you are good all the time but that you recognize there is a choice to be made. This makes sense to me. You can't just live. You have to stop and look and consider and choose and by choosing take hold of your life because your life is a thing, it is real, it does not have to exist. I almost wish I was under threat, that I would have to choose whether to run into the burning building or away. But that is not the way it works. The choice I have made is to walk dogs on the days I walk dogs. This is important.

Because what you thought just happened you chose to let happen. What you didn't do, you did.

What I didn't do, I did.

Often, despite my years here, despite this endless summer of work, I discover I don't know the city at all. I am stupidly amazed to find myself on a park in the wind, a view of the city, of all those windows of sun.

Accepting a great loss, without God, is hard. Everything is hard without God. Especially if you thought you believed in God because you went to church but found out all at once you did not.

Without God there is still the beauty of the world, but the problem is only God can equate the beautiful with the good. Without God all you have is the world and the night and the job and all these dogs. All you have is what you see and what you do.

I need to change my life. I know this. I am changing. I had friends and now I am alone. I used to drift through the days. No more drifting. I don't talk to many people these days because I am worrying and thinking all the time, which is new. But this is okay because I need to get through this. But thank God for the dogs. I need them. They pull me out of myself but not all the way. Being with them is like being in a purgatory between the world of people and the world of nothing-but-me. The dogs are sometimes human and sometimes not, but they are always alive and always need my attention. Attention is the important thing. If you look, really look, you can't help but see. Here is a creature who is not you who is terrified of the police siren two streets over. You are not alone.

I have walked dogs who knew the way and dogs who were afraid to go back into their own house. I have walked four cocker spaniels at once. I have been bitten on the lips by a golden retriever. I have asked dogs serious questions. I have accidentally wiped shit on my neck. I have dried a wet dog with a newspaper.

I have walked Maltese quiet and Maltese yippering-insane. Dogs I did not know have met me at the door with yelps of pleasure; dogs I did not know have huddled in corners and peed on the floor at my gentle approach. I have walked billions of labs — labs old and incontinent, labs young and tennis-ball obsessed, labs brown and white and black and mixed, every one full of random stupid ecstasy. I have walked a dog the size and shape of an otter that insisted on following me at a ten pace distance.

I have walked a well-trained Rottweiler who always peed on the same one lamppost and never seemed to be having any fun; I have walked an Irish Setter who insisted on sniffing at every doorstep, weird cigarette-smoking old lady leaning out of the screen-door or not. I have walked a giant sad drooling Great Dane and a young Cockapoo who raced around like a scribble.

I have seen two poofy-haired ladies coming out of a hair salon and getting into a great green car, laughing loudly, each carrying a Shih-Tzu with a red flower in its collar. I have seen an old man in a holey white-t-shirt watching with a general's pride his two Dobermans streaking circles around the park. I have seen paint splattered men carrying ladders laughing and talking in Spanish.

An old man in a beach chair once offered that he had a dog like that once who had face cancer. A drunk offered that he had helped build this house, this one right here. A woman behind a screen door told me I needed to drink more water.

I have seen giant cranes in motion. I have watched children play handball in the parking lot of a Baptist church.

I have smelled the alley. I have seen a giant woman hollering from the passenger window of a tiny car. I have allowed shirtless children with their warped-O accents pet the sullen husky. I have been lost on a staircase. I have seen a flock of young black boys on bicycles and the handlebars of each other's bicycles in the dusk swerving in an out of shocked traffic, their long white shirts flapping. I have seen grandmas sitting on benches together not talking. I have watched dozens of teenage boys playing football in the park at dusk, really playing, intricate and sudden bursts of action. I have seen men in jeans playing soccer on an overgrown field with no lines, their discarded shirts marking the goals. I have heard the sound of an ice cream truck (distorted by distance and speakers and motion and memory) that I did not see. I have seen great ships moving through the harbor like time passing. I have seen an old stooped man in plaid shorts carrying plastic bags full of something white. I have seen faded porcelain statues of Mary in windows facing the street. I have seen a license plate: "PLEASE."

How much I see and remember, even my despair. Perhaps that means this is not really despair. Perhaps that means this is a beginning rather than an end.

When I go in one hot afternoon to take care of the old blind dog it is the same — the dog lying perfectly still on his bed, facing away from the door, the stacked bright towels in the rocking chair, the bits of dust in the sunbeams. But something is different — the world has not changed, the world has changed.

I had to touch him to make sure.

The dogs are flying, just above the treetops of the park, just above the add-on gas-grill roof-decks of the city. Their front paws are splayed out before them, as if straining for purchase while skidding across a slick kitchen floor, but they are not straining. The dogs do not bark or drool or pant or swing their heads wildly from side to side, searching for unsuspecting squirrels to dive bomb. They are serious and purposeful as geese leaving for the winter. They are leaving forever. Their leashes trail behind and below them, streaming, unattached to any human hand.

A Weimaraner, healthy silver, young and smart, always slips her head under the curtain in the window when I come up the steps at the appointed time. She sees me and ducks away and I can hear her nails clicking on the tile floor as she wiggles herself nuts before I am even inside. She does not bark or hold the leash in her mouth and when I get inside and get the alarm code in she does not paw at the door or search my pockets for treats but sniffs at my stomach and wiggles and waits for me to press my face to hers and greet her.

Once, I sat on a bench for fifteen minutes and spoke to her with her head in my lap and stroked her fish-sleek sides. This dog knows me.

We often walk to the park. She is so easy, running her nose along the edge of the sidewalk, checking with me to see if it is okay to pause and investigate further.

By the baseball backstop in the park by the little pond, a handful of ducks. She sees them before I do, from a great distance, and begins to pull before I even know what she is pulling for.

She is like any other dog near such creatures. I hold tight to the leash, but she is also no other dog—what had been all love and calm is now all desperate desire. Though I hold the leash and would have held her, the collar snaps and she is gone.

There she is, in full sprint across the grass and the infield, a silver bolt, gone and so beautiful.

There is no reason to chase her, I think. I can only watch as the ducks sense her and explode apart into the air and as she keeps after them, out into the outfield toward the busy, unaware city street on the far side as the ducks fly higher and higher and she runs faster, as if she could strain herself into flight.

But then I am chasing her, screaming her name.

Before she reaches the street she releases the birds and turns and comes back to me.

The summer is not finished, not yet. There are still days. Whatever it means, it is not over, for which I am grateful.

STILLBORN
GIRAFFE

The summer before his junior year at college, Zack got a job as a cashier at the zoo. Often, because the other cashiers were desperate for air conditioning and because Zack felt that asking to work at a particular location was too close to acting like he cared, he worked outside, at a half-covered stand that sold overpriced key-chains and stuffed animals, along with food for giraffes — leafy stalks all the forest-green windbreakered zoo-people called "browse." You paid two bucks, then got to go around back to a deck where you could hold your stalk of browse out over the giraffe enclosure.

Zack didn't have any giraffe responsibilities. He just worked the register. He was supposed to ask every customer if she'd also like to renew or purchase a zoo membership, but he never did. There were a few different volunteers who worked out on the deck — their job was to attract wandering giraffes' attention by waving stalks of browse and calling out their names: Bowser, Wolverine, Juliet and Queenie. Zack had no idea how the volunteers could tell who was who.

It was just a job, a few hours standing braindead in

the thick heat. He decided he would never have children. Life was elsewhere, with his friends in cool carpeted basements, beside dark rivers.

On damp mornings, when the register was slow, just to do something, Zack would sometimes leave his post and go around back to look out at the giraffes. He liked how they moved. He liked their black eyes and the strength in their tongues. "They're not people," he caught himself thinking, more than once.

One night, high off someone's roommate's weed, lying on a soft black lawn looking up at a clouded sky, he said, "It's like, giraffes. They're just so, tall. You know?" Someone repeated what he'd said in a chipmunk voice and then everyone sprawled out around him was taken by helpless giggling, and then he was, too.

One gray Friday morning in early August, the end of summer still too far away to think about, Zack arrived at his post just before the zoo opened. It was too quiet. The Friday volunteer, Gary, a cheerful skinny old man with knobby knees and a sunburned-bright bald spot, was not vigorously sweeping the deck that never needed sweeping. Zack stood on the deck and looked across the empty patch of grass—the door to the giraffe barn had not even been opened.

As he turned back to his register a zoo-person, a round man in a forest green windbreaker zipped all the way up, quick-walked by, chatter from his clutched walkie-talkie trailing behind him. Not far behind, another zoo-person, a young woman Zack had watched give a demonstration to a pack of kids with a white owl perched on her gloved wrist. She'd been talking louder than she had to, and she had that over-enunciating nerd voice and the kids hadn't been paying attention just like he wouldn't have been paying attention. Now she wasn't wearing her glasses and her face was flushed and she was sort of pretty.

"What's going on?" he called out, surprising himself. The young woman snapped her head back, not slowing down.

"Queenie's giving birth," she said.

"She's pregnant?" he said. He found himself trotting after the young woman. She had strong, smooth legs. "Can I come?" he said. The young woman did not stop.

"She's really struggling. Just like all summer."

"Yup," said Zack. Stupid, he thought. She was almost running, and Zack only caught up to her as she was at the side door to the giraffe barn, and inside. He followed: a big round open room, gray day coming in from a big skylight, gray concrete floors, the smell of wet hay and shit. There were several stalls around the circumference, double rows of bars so you could see in but not reach in. Four of the stalls were occupied—three of the giraffes stood close to the bars, looking nowhere. In the fourth, the door open, a giraffe turned away, her front legs splayed out a little, as if she was holding herself up. The spindly legs of her calf were spilling out of her.

Zack felt a hand across his chest, and stopped—he'd been walking directly toward the giraffe. It was the young woman's hand. He saw that, in a line against the wall across from Queenie's stall, a handful of zoo-people in their forest green windbreakers, the man with the walkie-talkie, and Gary the volunteer, his mouth cracked open in pain.

Queenie swung her neck and turned as if to face them and as she did her legs splayed out further, and then one buckled and she sort of squatted forward into a helpless, awkward crouch. The line of zoo-people sucked in a breath; Gary whispered: "No."

Queenie regarded them with still black eyes.

"What is it?" whispered Zack.

"She has to get up," whispered the young woman, a teacher reprimanding a student. "That's too much weight on the baby."

"She's suffering," said another zoo-person.

The round zoo-person clicked off his walkie-talkie and passed it to the man next to him and stepped away from the group toward Queenie's stall, holding an open hand out towards her.

"Up," he said, plainly, neither kind nor unkind. Queenie regarded him with still black eyes. He was in her door. "Up," he said. And Queenie's long weird legs jerked to motion as if independent of her body. Her hooves pawed and slipped on the hay, but then found a grip. Inch by inch she hauled her long body up.

"There," said Gary.

And Queenie stood, turned and spread her front legs and then the calf's head was out and then, all at once, his shoulders, body, and spindly back legs tumbled onto the floor. He was still as a stretched out doll.

Blood and amniotic fluid splashed down. And then Queenie twisted and dipped her head, licked and tugged at the gunk and membrane covering her calf. The calf did not move.

Over the next weeks and months, Zack often felt the story of the stillborn giraffe in his mind, pressing to come out, with his friends in a car on the way to a party, with a girl with glitter in her hair on the riverbank in the near dark, with his roommates back at college. But he could not yet understand how to tell it. He felt somehow that he needed to hold onto what he'd seen and felt. How real death was. And then how the stillborn giraffe shuddered, and stretched, and lived.

DARK MOLLY

Dark Molly turns and the black smudged cross on her forehead is the color of her hair and her eyes and I have one of those moments when her eyes are my eyes and I have to close my eyes to get myself back and tell myself that she doesn't like you, moron.

When she's past me, the deep green of her skirt against the smooth backs of her thighs is a tingling in my ribs.

I open my eyes and see the pink flabby under-chin of the priest.

Jay's holding the brass bowl of black ash for the priest, staring at me with dead face and crossed eyes.

I don't give him the satisfaction of breaking up.

I watch the priest's black thumb.

I smell burning leaves.

The ash on the priest's thumb is gritty against my skin.

I whisper the words.

I can feel a warmth, as if the long dark hair of a girl is spreading down and in from the pit of my throat.

(It has always happened for me this way.)

I turn and see the other kids in line, their eyes hovering in the air.

Mr. Stinchcomb, on the back wall, is watching us, me, with folded arms.

I am not afraid of him because he is not Catholic and is only doing his job.

I wish for wings instead of hands — long gray dusty flaps, feathers trailing uselessly on the floor.

I would have to drink by dipping my face into a lake, a bowl, an oily puddle.

Not being able to touch another would make things easier.

And the flight.

Who wants these thick bones?

The knobs of Dark Molly's spine.

Other Molly, in the hall, asks if I am in one of my states.

Her forehead cross is distinct, two pinky-thick lines.

Her Death is a serious girl architect.

The backs of her hands are covered with blue ballpoint pen scribbles and she smells like shampoo.

I don't want her to die.

"Changed my pills," I say, which is what I say in such situations.

Other Molly should find me useless, but she is too good a girl.

"You have the stupidest doctors," she says.

"I don't care," I say.

Sometimes at night she goes down into the basement with Jay.

Later, he makes me smell his fingers.

I say "I'm okay," and she goes down the hall and I go down the stairs and there's the big window and wet black and green and orange woods and falling snow.

I wish a fox.

I want a cold cherry razorblade popsicle.

Through the door of English, another window, snow and the dead oak.

"We're out at noon," says Jay.

(He must have squirmed out of my ear and zipped on his face when I was in the falling snow.)

His fingers are black with ash.

"Come back from the Milky Way, bug eyes," he says.

"I've been here," I say.

"My mom's at her sister's," he says.

"Let's go to the movies," I say.

He's trying to grow a goatee and can't.

My ears turn into hands when I close my eyes as hard as I can.

There's a bluebird in the dead oak when the oak was alive.

Dark Molly is a hole carved in the air through to outerspace.

She's openly scrolling through text messages on her cellphone, will never get a detention.

She knows she's beautiful, that she's watched.

She looks out at the snow and the snow is the world is the inside of her mind.

The snow is not beautiful to her or to the world; it is happening.

Dark Molly is never cold.

The radiators hiss.

The snow has been injected into the soft underside of my wrists.

I'm buzzing for no reason.

I can't say I want to be different than I am.

It's difficult to pretend to be normal, but I make the effort and raise my hand to volunteer to read from Macbeth.

If only I could be a character and speak in poetry, sleep like a closed book, look up into wires and rope and ceiling panels and see stars and sky.

Then the principal's voice on the P.A. and we can stop pretending we aren't free.

Jay won't even let me bring my book bag with me.

He won't drive slow on the white soft streets so I keep the car on the road with my mind.

We need to be safe this day because Other Molly knows Dark Molly and so behind us is a Suburu full of girls, wild as released salmon, in short green skirts.

I wish the sudden black eyes of a deer in the white woods.

But only the mailboxes with erased names.

Jay's evil soul.

My wrong soul and the beauty of the girl.

The ash of Jay's cigarette drifts down onto his knee and he doesn't notice or doesn't care.

He hates rolling down the window so the inside of the car is Jay's gray mouth.

A country music song about fathers and daughters on so loud the speakers fuzz.

He wants to join the army but is worried about having to stop smoking pot.

Leaping from an airplane into nothing, the green and black wrecked world miles below.

Falling so fast you're not moving.

The screen door his mother had left open bangs in the wind.

All the lights on in the empty house.

Jay turns off the car and says "It's fuck Christmas."

"It's March," I say, as if I thought he thought it was Christmas.

He believes I'm spacier than I am, but I've always got at least a few fingers in the earth.

Though sometimes I have to hold on.

Snow like billions of silent electric punctuation marks.

A breath of the cold clean air.

Standing by the car on their narrow, nervous deer-feet in the snow: Other Molly and Kaitlyn — braces and big tits and a smirk — and Dark Molly.

Dark Molly alone has wiped the ash from her forehead.

She catches my eye and I look away.

I wish to free the creature, green and translucent and warm, that is coalescing beneath my breastbone.

The feeling is close to what happens when I eat the body, but it can't be from God.

Maybe it's all just radio waves read wrong.

Inside we throw off our shoes and coats and the girls pull away their sweaters and Jay and I tear off our ties and Jay turns on the Food network loud and we go down into the basement.

Glass jars of screws, the smell of laundry, the windows at the tops of the concrete walls black with snow.

A ratty plaid couch, an old recliner, a bare light bulb bright as the idea of an orange.

Other Molly wants a sleeve of yellow cheese.

Kaitlyn opens an Old Milwaukee.

Dark Molly leans back into the couch, dark smooth legs crossed, gazing up with a blank face and deep blank brown eyes over my shoulder at Jay's closed hand.

He opens a handful of what could be baby teeth.

We swallow the teeth with beer and orange juice.

I pour vodka and Sprite into a Star Wars glass and hand it to Dark Molly and she looks up at me with her dark blank eyes and says, "Do I want this?"

"I love you," I say and she is not surprised but takes the glass.

We are all lying in the snow.

Water drips up my spine.

I see in the mirror the ash cross still black on my forehead, forever, but my eyes are gone.

Other Molly goes into the video game.

Clocks blink.

Jay is sitting on the lip of the tub, no shirt on, staring out the window at the snow and the night whispering sadly: "I am going to fuck the shit out of brace-face."

"Don't be a baby," he says.

"It's time to grow up," he says.

His ash cross is a black smear.

I can hear the snow falling and I can see there is a pattern that I could understand if I spent the night.

But Dark Molly sits in the green recliner in the pink room holding the empty Star Wars glass in her lap with both hands.

Jay and Kaitlyn are trapped in a closet in the basement, howling.

Outside, the falling snow glows.

Dark Molly says: "Do you believe in eternal life?"

"I do," I say.

She smiles and sets the glass at her feet and stands and moves through the snow and stands before me.

"Do you believe in eternal life?" I say.

My fingers are against the side of her face, her burning ear, and she shivers.

"Someone just walked over my grave," she says, and licks her thumb and rubs the ash from my forehead.

She shows me her black thumb and slips her thumb between my lips.

Ash, and lemonade, and flesh warm with blood.

She leans in closer and is almost touching my chest with the tips of her breasts and she whispers: "You're about to die."

A GIRL CALLED RANDOM

The woman who opened the white-wreathed front door was wearing a bright yellow shirt that Scott imagined would feel like burlap and a necklace of linked silver fish the size of real minnows. She was very thin and had long soft silver hair and was not wearing makeup. She was, thought Scott, like no one I have ever known.

The woman opened her mouth in naked astonishment as she opened her arms to Scott's wife, Corinne. "Little Cory Dougherty! Look at you!" she said.

"Hi Missus Hansen," said his wife, opening her arms just enough so they wouldn't be crushed inside the embrace. It was unlike his wife to be so half-hearted; on the other hand, she had been unusually quiet all day, ever since they'd arrived in Baltimore. She didn't even meet his eyes over Mrs. Hansen's shoulder to share her surprise, or annoyance, or disdain.

"Oh, please, dear," said Mrs. Hansen, pulling her head back and looking down her nose at Corinne in mock disapproval. "'Missus Hansen,' 'Missus Hansen.' Call me Margot."

"Okay Missus Hansen," said Corinne.

"Margot," she said.

"Margot," said Corinne.

"Now," said Mrs. Hansen, releasing her and training her attention on Scott, "Is this the fine young man who has taken you away from us?"

The Hansen's Christmas party was an annual tradition in Roland Park in Baltimore, where Corinne grew up, but Scott had never been. When they were first serious, Scott's grandmother was about to die and then, the Christmas after they were married, she died. The next few Christmases there was always a reason to stay up north—a new niece, work late on Christmas Eve. Not that Corinne argued forcefully for a Christmas trip to Baltimore—summers and Thanksgivings were enough. They were only at her old house this Christmas because they'd missed Thanksgiving to visit college friends in Ann Arbor, so her mother had insisted.

They'd been hoping to have good news about a baby.

It was not time to panic. Scott said this over and over. And Corinne made jokes about the price of a flight to China, about ridiculous names they might never be able to even pretend to contemplate: a boy called Circle. A girl called Random.

She said she'd be okay no matter what. But he'd seen the sheet of graph paper she'd folded into her journal, each square filled with perfect green and orange and red numbers and letters that represented some condition of some part of her body. She couldn't even figure out what to tip at a restaurant.

They were waiting for some test results. He did not have a good feeling.

The first night in Baltimore, over glass goblets of thick red wine and herby lamb, her mother had mentioned casually that they were thinking of remodeling the extra room on the third floor as a library. Or a nursery.

Scott woke up the next morning to see his wife kneeling before her old dollhouse that took up half the wall, poking at the tiny, delicate furniture. The dollhouse had been left complete — little rooms full of little tables and chairs and beds and clocks and books that opened and lamps that worked. But there were no people. And there were not enough stairs and hallways. The rooms were complete, but not connected.

The houses in Roland Park were older and larger and more expensive than the houses Scott had known growing up. Porches, shingles, strangely shaped windows. The houses were also closer to each other and closer to the road. They had small back and side yards separated from each other by exotic bushes and sturdy wooden fences. There were sidewalks. There were trees as old as the houses with branches that arched a canopy over the narrow street, which was always crammed with parked cars because not many of the houses had garages.

Corinne had led Scott up and down the alleys, pointed out backyards, talked about this one with a son at Princeton, this one where the drunken doctor lived. Scott counted the alarm system signs.

The neighborhood was more or less an enclave of rich white people in the middle of the poor black city. An island of big old houses and trees in the middle of a sea of endless rows of brick and gray formstone rowhouses.

At any time of day or night, a raving siren traced the edge of the neighborhood and disappeared.

The house of the party was tree-trunk brown with dark green trim and every window was full of light. In the patch of front yard, dusted with snow, a sheet metal giraffe. Paper lanterns with real burning candles inside hung on the front porch. More furniture on the porch than in his parents' living room.

Inside were bare golden wood floors covered here and there by well worn but still luxurious Oriental rugs. Bookcases. Track lighting.

There was music — "Santa Claus is Coming to Town" by Bruce Springsteen — coming from hidden speakers.

The house was already mostly full. The people were nothing like the people Scott had grown up with. Two bearded men in Hawaiian shirts holding cups of wine pointed at and loudly appraised aspects of the molding. The women were wearing bright or sharp or fuzzy necklaces. Children from catalogs — boys like tiny mountain climbers, girls with bright things clasping their shiny hair into asymmetric waves — darted here and there. A few teenagers huddled in opposite corners and stared into their phones.

Along one wall, in front of a long window a sofa must have been moved away from, stood the bar — a door laid atop two ordinary sawhorses with an optical-illusion-shimmery lined-green tablecloth thrown over it. There were stacks and stacks of plastic cups, as at a frat party, but also a silver bowl of ice with silver tongs. There were maybe a dozen bottles of wine, all opened. There was Maker's Mark and Bombay Sapphire and Grey Goose and something with golden Russian letters on the label. On the floor under the bar, bottled beers buried in open coolers full of ice.

Before a word was out of his mouth, he was being led by Corinne towards the bar, which was not how things usually went. Scott stood mute next to her, watching her twirl the wine bottles to read the labels. She decided on sloshing vodka into cup which she then reddened with a little cranberry juice. Then she plunked in a hunk of ice from the beer cooler.

She bent over to take a sip of her drink so it wouldn't spill.

"I thought you wanted to pop in and pop out," said Scott.

"I said I maybe didn't want to stay all that long," she said.

"That's not what you said," said Scott. "I thought you didn't want to come."

"I didn't," said Corinne.

"I feel weird," said Scott.

"What do you mean *you* feel weird? Are you suddenly surrounded by people who knew you when you were ten?"

"I don't know why. I guess just all this stuff. This neighborhood."

"You've been to my parents' house before," she said.

"And I feel weird there, too," he said, whispering.

"Are you afraid of books?" she said, not whispering at all.

"I'm afraid of your Dad's stuffed birds," he said, whispering.

"I went to your Christmas," she said sharply. The music was just loud enough that no one looked.

"Keep your voice down," said Scott carefully.

"Why?" she said.

"What got into you?"

"Nothing."

"I don't see why you're bitching at me. You don't want to be here either."

"Grow up, Scotty."

"You want to be here?"

"We're here now."

"I don't want to get drunk," said Scott.

"I don't care. I'm not your mother," she said.

"Fine. I'll have a drink."

"Be my guest," she said.

"Fine," he said, and dipped over to tub to dig through the ice for a beer that didn't look too dark or thick or sweet, coming up with a Moose Juice — abstract purple antlers on the label.

When he stood up, Corinne was gone.

There was nothing for it but stand there and drink the beer and try not to look out of place, but he didn't see a bottle opener. He looked among the liquor bottles and the wine bottles and the cups; he looked on the floor near the tubs of ice. After he craned his head over the bar to look behind it and was considering knocking the cap off against the edge of the bar, Margot Hansen appeared at his side.

"Can I help you find something?" she said, tilting

her head like a third-grade teacher. Words disappeared from Scott's mouth and he helplessly mimed the action of opening a bottle, though he'd left his beer sitting on the bar. Margot watched him with alarm gathering in her eyes.

"Uh. The opener. The bottle opener," said Scott finally, seizing his beer.

"Right here," said Margot, handing him a silver slab of metal that had been resting on the table next to his beer.

"Ah," said Scott, taking the slab of silver metal. "Thank you."

"Certainly," said Margot. "Enjoy." She melted away into the party as Scott studied the slab and found the groove and teeth underneath and fit it to the bottle to snap the cap free.

When he turned his wife was still nowhere among the pockets of brightly attired adults with children scrambling among them. He was totally alone — at least Corinne's parents hadn't yet arrived (not that they were awful, but he always had the sense that they were making too deliberate an effort to appear interested in the trials and tribulations of whatever software manual he was working on). He could smell, very faintly, the rich sweet scent of expensive pot — someone had it on their clothes. Probably someone who should be paying more attention to their kids, he thought. He hated these people for making him think like his parents.

He needed to drink.

He tipped the beer to his lips — it was thick and sweet, just as he'd tried to avoid. Nothing for it now. He took a half-bottle slurp as he took a few steps away from the bar and found himself standing in front of what seemed to him a spread-out and pressed-flat framed toddler's dress. The intricate detail was astonishing: red and brown dyed cloth, streaks of blue, beads and stones sewn in with bright red thread.

It was almost a shame to see something so beautiful in a frame on a wall, so far away from where it must have been made. Still, thought Scott, he would rather own something so beautiful than inherit, for example, his mother's giant-eyed-baby-angel china.

He realized without turning his head that he was not the only one studying the framed dress.

"Bill brought that back from Tibet," said his companion.

"Bill?" said Scott.

"Bill. I'm sorry. Bill Hansen. The house we're in now."

"I see," said Scott, thinking, who says I see? How old am I? "What is it?"

"It's a child's prayer shawl. It's used in some religious ceremony or other. He explained it to me once." Scott glanced at his companion: a tall man, possibly in his fifties, with a big face and nose that he tipped up just enough so Scott could see into his wide dark nostrils. His hair was graying but also thick with waves and his black eyeglasses floated in his hair like a boat. "Have you had a chance," he continued, "to see the circumcision masks?"

"No," said Scott. "Not yet."

"They're in the kitchen, if you get a free second."

"In the kitchen?"

"Just above the sink. They're really something. You'll

notice how the themes of the kitchen are based on the colors of the masks."

"I'm Scott," said Scott, offering his hand. "I'm Corinne's boyfriend. I mean husband." That was strange, he thought

"Corinne?" said the tall man, taking Scott's hand tentatively in his big knotty dry hand.

"Corinne," said Scott. "Corinne Dougherty."

"Of course, of course," said the tall man, suddenly gripping Scott's hand much harder. "Cory Dougherty."

"That's her," said Scott, letting his big hand go.

"Did you meet at college?"

"Yup."

"It wasn't so long ago she was a just a little girl. Just a little dark ghost."

"A ghost?" said Scott.

"That must sound a bit morbid. It's really a term of endearment. She was just the sort of child who was always hovering around the edges, by herself. Very quiet."

"Really?" said Scott thinking, maybe this guy had the wrong girl. On the other hand, it's not like he knew her when she was a kid

"You never could tell what was going on in her head," said the tall man. "And then, of course, after the accident. We were all so worried."

Scott had no idea what he was talking about. He studied the prayer shawl furiously, tracing one thread from the collar to the shoulder and back. He couldn't think of anything to say. He tried not to change his facial expression as he could sense his companion had turned to look him over.

"I'm sure you know all about that," said the tall man carefully.

"Oh yeah," said Scott.

The tall man turned back to the prayer shawl and immediately raised his cup to his lips and tipped whatever golden liquid was left there into his mouth. The tall man was not fooled. He swallowed and his giant Adam's apple bobbed as if he was swallowing a fist-sized rock.

"Well. Good. I'm glad she turned out well," said the tall man.

"She did," said Scott.

"Isn't the beadwork incredible? Nothing like it in our world."

"No," said Scott. The tall man looked into his empty cup.

"Seems I need a refill. Good to meet you, then. Matt?"

"Scott," said Scott, offering his hand.

"Good. Scott," he said, taking Scott's hand, "Remember those circumcision masks." Then the tall man drifted off, not towards the bar, but in the other direction. Scott realized he'd never learned his name. He watched the tall man pause to greet a tall woman in a pixie haircut with a little boy hanging onto the bottom of her black dress just as a short goateed man in a tux burst in from the other room grinning with his arms spread, wearing a light-up Rudolph nose. A woman in a scratchy orange scarf breezed by Scott carrying a giant shimmering copper pot full of something bright yellow.

He could not have felt more lost in another country. Where was his wife? And what was the accident?

For lack of anywhere to go, he followed the woman with the copper pot into the dining room.

Corinne was not in the dining room.

The dining room table was almost overflowing with food in strange, colorful pots and platters. A great white bowl of shrimp flecked with red and green. A black cauldron with a lid. A sea-green plate of what seemed to be giant crispy tortellini. Gleaming asparagus.

Scott snatched a roll from a reedy basket and bit into it — the roll was soft and still warm, but dotted with strange bitter seeds.

The walls of the dining room were nearly covered by framed photographs. Many were black and white — a close-up of the eye of a fly; farmers covering their eyes with their forearms against the sun; a child's chalk drawing on a sidewalk; a noble face with big dark eyes and a precise smirk. A few color prints: green vines climbing a gravestone and, Scott was shocked to see, a wobbly-looking thin-armed boy soldier holding a dangling gun the size of his leg.

Scott's mom and dad had a framed oval portrait of his grandmother when she was young, a big posed family portrait from J.C. Penny, a few prints of sailboats, a poster of the Boston skyline with the name of the city in Red Sox colors along the bottom.

He needed another drink.

Corinne was not at the bar. He drained what was left of the Moose Juice and could not see where the empties went so he set the bottle on the flat silver base of a snaking tube of a lamp. He took another bottle at random from the cooler, a dragon smoking a cigar on the label, and he opened it with the flat silver slab. It tasted clear and red; not bad. He drained the dragon beer and set it on the base of the lamp next to the Moose Juice, then picked out and opened another.

There were more people now, and the conversation was louder than the music, a bluegrass version of "God Rest Ye Merry Gentlemen" fading into some sort of piercing nasal chanting. A little girl in a forest-green smock at his feet was trying to draw on the ancient rug with a red crayon. He couldn't imagine having a child. What were you supposed to say if you found your kid trying to draw on your expensive foreign rug?

"What are you drawing?" he said.

"I'm not drawing," said the little girl, not looking up. "I'm digging."

"I see," said Scott.

He had to find his wife.

Corinne was not in the dimly lit carpeted basement with the almost-teenagers sprawled on puffy white couches watching one of the reality shows about rich California teenagers crying in glittery dresses. Scott might have merely headed back up the stairs if the kids had not all turned as one to face him, like a warren of prairie dogs.

"Don't you have Toy Story or something?" said Scott, to say something.

"Toy Story is gay," said one boy with shiny blond hair in his eyes, turning back to the TV, as they all did, having assessed Scott as just another clueless adult.

"Toy Story is awesome," said Scott, but none of the kids responded.

He barked a shin on a crate of vodka on his way to the stairs up.

Corinne was not in the bathroom with the flickering candles in jeweled glass bowls. But, among the candles near the sink, a half-full cup of what looked like the weak pink of vodka with a splash of cranberry juice. Corinne had abandoned her drink. It was not like her.

She was also not in the kitchen. The circumcision masks were indeed hung in a row over the sink, and the walls were painted the same peculiar burnt red as the beads that made the masks' mouths. Interspersed among the masks were giant frames of white paper at the center of which were tiny black and white photographs of flowers. On the other side of the kitchen, between windows, pots and pans dangled on chains. Tile the color of the desert. A shelf of little glass jars full of spices. A silver refrigerator and a silver sink and a silver dishwasher.

A few women stood at the island stove in the center of the room, gazing into a pan full of oily dark meat, debating temperatures.

Margot Hansen swept in with an armful of white lilies. She opened an overhead cabinet, pawed through it with her free hand, and then spied Scott.

"Can I get you something?" she asked with her hand in the cabinet.

"No, sorry," said Scott. "I was just looking for Corinne."

"You've got to keep a closer eye on her than that," she said.

"That's what I hear," said Scott. Margot, up on her toes, reached further into the cabinet, clinking glasses.

"God damn," she said.

"Do you need help?" said Scott.

"I just might. There's a vase just back there...." Scott stepped around the women cooking and reached up into the cabinet and pulled out the glass vase. He was relieved to see it was not etched in hieroglyphics or ringed with gold leaf. It was an ordinary glass vase.

"Do you want water in here?" said Scott.

"That would be lovely," she said. Scott filled the vase halfway up with water and set it on the woodblock counter and Margot poked the stems of the lilies in. Scott watched her fluff at the greens, tug a few flowers a few millimeters to distribute them evenly. Lilies were his mother's favorite flower. "Are you having a good time?" asked Margot, concentrating, her fingers among the flowers.

"Sure," said Scott.

"You're just a little lost," she said.

"I'm just a little lost."

"I wouldn't worry," she said, looking up. "Just have another drink and it will pass."

"Okay," said Scott.

"In the meantime, maybe you could set these flowers out for me?"

"No problem," said Scott. "Where do you want them?"

"Wherever seems best, my dear. And if your wife still hasn't appeared, you might try outside."

"Outside?"

"The back deck. If she's the same girl she was, that would be my best guess."

Scott took up the lilies and carried them out of the kitchen, petals brushing against his chin and neck, into the room with the liquor and the music, which had flipped from the nasal chanting to plain old "White Christmas."

Corinne's parents had arrived.

Scott stood in the doorway holding the lilies watching Corinne's father purse his lips in absurd concentration as he poured white wine into two plastic cups while his wife talked to another woman with dangling, rusty-looking earrings, making the same sweeping gestures with her hands that Corinne would have made.

It was strange that Corinne never wanted to come home because she loved her parents and they loved her; that was clear. She talked to them on the phone much more often than he talked to his parents. Just that morning they'd surprised her with her old rock collection resurrected from the basement—all the rocks still clearly labeled in their places in the plastic tackle box: a few geodes, agates, hematite, pyrite, calcite, sulfur, tiger-eye. She'd made Scott quiz her on all the rocks by blindfolding her with the sleeves of an old grey sweatshirt and then handing her each rock, one by one—she knew every rock. She'd already put the tackle box next to her bag to take home, even though she'd have to carry it on the plane.

Corinne's excitement at seeing her old rocks again was who he knew her as. But the handwriting on the labels in the tackle box, eerily straight and perfect, like in the squares of the sheet of folded graph paper in her journal, was not. Neither did the idea of Corinne as a ghost make any sense to him. They'd met at a bar when she'd butted in to an argument he was having with his friends about politics.

"I didn't realize the genius convention was tonight," she'd said from the next booth. She was alone, her girls had gone to the bathroom. All his buddies could do was halt and gawk. She was wearing a low-cut sky-blue tank top and she'd lined her eyes into cat's eyes.

"You're late," said the five jack-and-cokes in Scott's veins.

Scott spied the door out to the deck in the back of the room and, looking into the lilies as he walked, careful not to make eye contact with Corinne's parents, he darted through the loud, crowded room, avoiding the crayon-on-the-rug little girl charging across his path with a dump truck.

He stepped outside into the wet sparkling-foggy cold—he hadn't realized how warm it was inside—and closed the door behind him.

The deck was not large, but there was enough space for a gas grill and a small table with chairs. A tub of ice and a box of white wine in the corner. White lights strung in spirals around the deck railing. A few steps down to a still-thick and mostly green back lawn that spread out several dozen feet to the tall shrubs that bordered the alley. A little dead garden in the corner of the lawn. A birdbath. A lacrosse goal.

And, as still as the night, Corinne, sitting at the table without her coat, in her lap a spread open copy of Where the Wild Things Are. She did not turn when the door opened or when the door closed.

Scott saw that something was about to happen.

He set the vase of lilies on the table before his wife.

"I got these for you," he said.

"You did not," said Corrine, not unkindly, though she didn't look up from her book.

"I've been looking everywhere."

"I've been right here," she said. The book was open to the scene of Max and the creatures beginning their wild rumpus. No words. She did not turn the page.

The noise of the party from the house through the window seemed like it was coming from far away. He had the sensation of being underwater, floating, looking in through the windows at the ordinary people talking, breathing air. He saw that Corinne had had to position herself and the book just so to be able to read in the light from the party.

"I heard some stories about you," he said.

"Yeah?" she said, looking up.

"What was the accident?"

"The accident," she said. She smiled, glanced back at the party. The party was a different world.

"I heard something about an accident," said Scott.

"What do you expect me to say?" said Corinne.

"I don't know, Corinne. Jesus. I can't believe you never told me."

"When I was little I stole my dad's car," she said. Her voice was oddly flat.

"You stole your dad's car? How old were you?"

"I don't know. Eleven. We had some fight about not letting me go out on my bike at night. So I just waited until they were asleep and took the keys."

"And you crashed it."

"I crashed it. I didn't get very far. Right into the back of a minivan. Broke my arm, though. Wrecked the car."

"I can't believe you never told me."

"It's no big deal."

"Yes it is."

"I know. I know. I guess when I didn't tell you. I guess I just kept not telling you."

There was a wave of laughter from inside the house.

"It's just so weird," said Scott.

"I know."

"I can't even imagine you doing that."

"Me neither," said Corinne.

"I mean, were you depressed?"

"I don't know. I was just a kid."

"So that's it then? No reason?"

"That's it. That's the accident. That's why they call it an accident. It's not like it has any effect on my life now."

"Then why didn't you tell me?"

"I don't know," she said. A giant truck rumbled by along the edge of the neighborhood. Another wave of laughter from inside. A dog barked somewhere across the alley.

"I feel weird here," said Scott, looking at the lilies, their white standing out sharply against the dark yard. "I feel totally out of place."

"You'd better give me a baby," said Corinne suddenly.

His wife turned to look at him. Her eyes were very green. She was very beautiful. He could not imagine her as a child. He could not imagine her as a mother.

But he could see their child. A girl. She has his wife's green eyes. She is sitting at his feet at the edge of the ocean, scrawling her name in the hard wet sand with a shard of a seashell.

"I'll do what I can," he said.

"I'm not fucking around," she said. "I'm serious. If we can't have a baby I'm going to fall apart."

Scott felt a hollowness open in the center of his chest. He was standing on a stranger's deck in an alien city. He saw that he did not know his wife and that he loved her. And that he had no control over their lives.

"I'm not fucking around either," he said and sank down into the chair beside her and looked at the lilies, so white and alive in the cold. He saw the vase of lilies in his mother's white kitchen.

"I lied," she said.

"You lied," he said.

"I didn't have a fight with my dad before I stole his car. I just got this idea in my head. I just wanted to steal it. I wanted to run away."

"I want to run away right now," he said.

"Me too," said Corinne.

They sat together in the dark and cold, listening to the music and voices from the bright house.

I WON THE
BRONZE MEDAL

I did not want to walk into 7–11 in the middle of the night barefoot, but I got into an argument with my mother. My mother says she is dying. I hate my mother. "You know where the butter is," she says. This is in a room without windows. You have to know some other things to understand. She is not really dying, and I do not hate her. I just wanted breakfast.

I used to love to drink coffee. I could punch trees. Now coffee makes me too nervous. Sometimes there is too much coffee in the decaf coffee. Karl does not believe me, no matter how many times I tell him. Karl works the late shift at 7-11 and his name is Vishad. He reminds me very much of Karl who was my coach. Karl has a black mustache and is sometimes not happy with me but he always looks me in the eyes. Fuck you if you are cruel to Karl.

I am sorry for cursing. Sometimes I cannot help myself. I can't stand it when babies cry in the grocery store. I hear their crying right in the center of my skull, just above my uvula. It's like I swallowed a butterfly. I have never actually swallowed a butterfly, but I have swallowed a moth. What happens behind my skull when I hear a baby crying in the grocery store is bigger and more colorful and less hairy than when I swallowed a moth. Fuck you if you do not think the difference between swallowing a butterfly and swallowing a moth is important.

I am sorry for cursing. I am not angry out of anger. I do not hate anyone, even the boy who leaned out of the window of the silver truck to toss a crushed beer can in my direction. What a stupid thing to throw—how could anyone control it? And yes, stranger, I did know that I wasn't wearing shoes.

Who has never once forgotten to put on their shoes before leaving the house? I usually remember. And it's not like I was planning to walk to Annapolis—I was just going for a drive.

Driving calms me and would calm me even more if Maryland would let us drive faster. Cars are more controllable than missiles and look how many of those we have. It's also stupid that they want to phase out cassette tapes.

But I'm not angry about it. I'm not. I love to have a good conversation. I am always willing to help out if you get your car stuck in the snow. I keep a shovel just inside the front door and when it snows I watch out the window to see if anyone needs help. Someone could have stopped to give me a ride—anyone could see I didn't have shoes. But I can't complain—when I got into 7-11 Karl took one look at me and reached down below the counter to grab me a handful of paper towels. Karl is a kind man. I told him he was a kind man.

"My name is Vishad," he said. I cannot make Karl understand that I call him Karl as a gesture of respect. I respect Karl so much that if someone were to harm him

I would immediately walk into the kitchen. That's where the knives are.

I would give my bronze medal to Karl. I hang it from a nail on the wall in my room. My mother bought me an expensive frame so I hung the frame on the wall, too, next to the medal. I don't like the idea of putting things in other things.

"Why did I spend money on that?" says my mother every day. She says this so I will forget to ask her to make me breakfast so, when I remember, I ask her to make me breakfast and she says no. Sometimes she says she wishes I had never won the medal in the first place, which means she wants me to do my laundry. I don't mind doing the laundry—the dryer knocks in a nice rhythm when it gets unbalanced. I love my mother and fuck you if you don't know why.

I love my mother but I was angry. I admit it. I was very hungry and she would not make me breakfast. She said she was asleep. It was past midnight so it was morning but she didn't believe me. I can see that I could have been more considerate. She loves me. She does not mind when she is watching a program and I put in a COPS on tape.

In my favorite a police car drives into a forest and catches on fire. The cop gets out and watches his car burn and he holds onto the fire extinguisher that did not work. Like him I always want people to understand me. I was angry because my mother didn't want to make me breakfast and she never wants to make me breakfast even though she knows I always turn the burners up too high and burn the eggs and then I eat them right out of the pan and burn my fingers and my mouth.

I wanted to get to 7-11 early enough to wait for Barry who brings the newspapers in the big green truck and slips me old papers so I can read up on all the news without having to pay. There is nothing wrong with reading the news a day late — you just have to get used to it, like daylight savings time. One day later the news gets more real, like the way a Polaroid starts out as nothing and then burns into what it is. I like to take photographs of our street when it rains so hard the drains can't keep up. I have always wanted the city to flood so I could float down our street. I bought an inflatable raft a long time ago. I keep it in the basement and my mother does not know it is there.

I have a Playboy in the closet. I keep the leftover Halloween candy in my ice skates until I eat it all. If I go slow I can make it last until Christmas. My mother has cigarettes in her perfume drawer. I count them every few days. There are always eleven. I find cigarette smoking a disgusting habit. I am simple. The idea of interfering with breath makes no sense to me. Who knows when you will need as much breath as you can get? What if there is someone chasing you? I believe in being prepared.

I know it was stupid to get into a car without shoes and I know it was stupid to let the car run out of gas. I don't always do what I know is right when I have a strong feeling. There are tiny pieces of glass all over the sidewalks. I had to walk very carefully. It was good that it rained because rain makes concrete softer. I don't mind cold. I can staple my thumb.

I felt lonely. I admit it. Which is why I went in to see Karl, even though I did not have any money. There was not even enough change in the glove box for a hot dog. I only eat hot dogs to be friendly to Karl. I get energy from bananas and oatmeal and when my mother cooks me breakfast. She insists I not help her in the kitchen but sit at the table and wait. She asks me if I want orange juice and then does not bring me the orange juice. She never wants to cook breakfast anymore. Do it yourself, she says. You are a grown man. I bring up the check I get every month from Maryland for when the garbage truck broke my leg and made it different for me to walk. She says you just keep bringing that up. I don't know why I let you go away to Colorado when you were just a boy. I wish I'd never let you go. Then I wouldn't have won the bronze medal, I say. I should have never let you go to Colorado, she says. I learned everything in Colorado, I say. Why don't you go back there, then, she says. Get someone out there to cook you breakfast in the middle of the night. If that's the way you feel maybe I will go, I say, and leave. You'll need shoes in Colorado, she says. No, I won't, I say.

I wasn't just being difficult. I knew at that moment that I wouldn't need shoes. It's interesting how my brain can get overloaded. Once I walked into a bunch of pigeons and when they took off all around me I couldn't stop myself from going after all of them. They were like grey butterflies in my brain. I caught one. I have superior reflexes. I put the pigeon down and he was fine.

Karl does not like it when I try to scare the birds away from the front of 7-11, even though it is for the best. Birds are dirty things. I would do anything for Karl. One night I came in late and I did not have the dollar I thought I had in my shoe so he went back into the little room behind the register and came out with a white bowl that had some rice in it and something orange and brown that sort of looked like diarrhea. It was good substantial food even though it looked like diarrhea. Karl acted like he was mad when I told him it looked like diarrhea even though I ate it all and it was good.

I would do anything for Karl. Whenever I tell him this he tells me his name is Vishad. I can't make him understand how much I respect him and how much I appreciate the way he always looks me in the eyes.

He looked me in the eyes as I was standing in the 7-11 barefoot handing him the dirty paper towels he said to me "I am very sorry but I must ask you to please leave my store."

"I'll be normal in five minutes," I said.

"I'm sorry but please understand me. I must ask you to leave my store or I must call the police. "

"I'm not any trouble," I said.

"Please. I have been receiving complaints. I have my responsibilities. I have a family," he said.

"I have a mother," I said.

"I am very sorry, please understand," he said.

"You don't have to worry about me, Karl. I promise. I promise you so much," I said. I said it just that way— "I promise you so much." I will never forget exactly what I said. I remember it good now because I just said it.

I could have done a lot of things but I believe that life is a series of moments to be mastered. But I won. I walked right out of 7-11 into the wet. That's why I'm here. Because of my shoes. It's not so weird. But why are you here?

The light from these streetlights — it looks white

enough from here but if you saw it from a plane it would look orange. One day I will fly on a plane again. I won the bronze medal. The platform I stood on to get it made me taller than the man with glasses who put the medal around my neck. I looked up and listened to the Swedish National Anthem which is a good song about wanting to live in the North and being ancient. I once took a bus to the library to ask a librarian about the words and she was very helpful. I did not even need to tell her I won the bronze medal. I only told her after. People in Barcelona walk too close to you. The Swedish boy who beat me smelled like chalk and barf and had cauliflower ears. He was little but he was better than me. I had him wrapped up but he did not move off his center and I could not make myself wait and I held him too hard and he reversed. It was the one moment I did not master. The next boy I wrestled was from Japan and I was so angry I kept imagining he was trying to whisper something into my ear and then I had him. It was something. I picked him up and whirled him around and even though I had him and I had my feet on the mat I felt like I was throwing myself into the air.

I love my mother and I love Karl, who once told me I had the strongest hands in the world.

Karl, I will not give up.

JOHN'S STORY

Here's my brother John a few years from now.

He's a little taller, still growing, thin and bony even though he only takes in Coke and millions of ice cream sandwiches his mom buys special. His hair is still spiky and dyed black.

He's quiet and folded in, but not at peace. When he is forced to speak — to his parents, to his teachers, to some ball-capped kid at school holding a conversation in front of the soda machine oblivious to John standing there waiting — it comes out in a trembling burst, angry and out-of-control even when he isn't. His parents hear the tone and threaten, his teachers stop calling on him, the ball-capped kid rolls his eyes and smirks and gets out of the way and makes a joke about him to the girl he's talking to and the girl, not unkind, green eyes, nice ass, whaps the guy on the shoulder and says come off it, as if John is only a little brother. This is the worst part. John feels stunted, small. And, more than anything else, alone.

John sometimes tells himself he is not meant for this random town in Massachusetts, but when he really looks hard at his life and the world, at his parents going to work and making dinner and watching TV, at his older brother the golden child with his scholarship skating through college and then moving to the city, at the kids at school with their cars and parties, at the goth kids lounging around the Smoothie Hut at the mall, at the old white churches with the booming new bells, at the young men struggling stoically against the war in the bright dusty cities on television, at his towns' narrow winding roads that eventually lead anywhere, he admits to himself that the problem isn't the world, isn't everybody else, it's him. Everybody else seems to be able to get by in a way that makes sense. He imagines suicide by tearing down one of the winding roads at top speed and letting the car lose the road where it wanted to. Mostly these thoughts aren't serious, but every now and then he catches himself — it would be so easy, just a second, like opening a closed hand.

It's not as if he is black-hearted or even that different. He follows the Red Sox like everybody else (though he does it alone, at his computer). And though he keeps mostly to himself, he has friends, computer-guys who stay up late playing sword-and-sorcery games together over the internet, weirdo-guys with intricate ball-point pen tattoos and black hooded sweatshirts who he tags along with to local emo-or-punk-or-hardcore-or-whatever shows. He loves he blind crying-screaming-singing of the singers, the obliteratingly loud weeping chainsaw of the music. He understands it, loses himself in it. For a few minutes there is the music and only the music and he is part of it and everybody in that place listening is part of him. He loves the pit. He doesn't mind the bruises. If he falls, the seething mass reaches out hands to help him up. He even kisses a girl once in the sweaty confusion just after, and she is high, and he never gets her name, but still; it is a kiss. Every night of the spring before graduation he goes over the kiss in his mind: he knows exactly how tall she is, her forehead at his nose; the sharp smell of citrus and hay in that dank basement.

He tries to teach himself the guitar. He listens to music on his headphones late at night; he wakes up in the morning and drinks a can of Coke and goes to school. The days go on. He thinks maybe he will go to community college, find some job in computers, then an apartment. It's something, he tells himself.

He doesn't really believe he has enlisted until he tells his parents during dinner. His mom's fried chicken and Rice-a-Roni. It is only then he understands in his mother's shock, in her trembling demand to march back to that recruiting officer and take it back, how desperate he is, how far he is willing to go.

He refuses his mother's demand with a new firmness, not screaming or complaining, simply saying no and looking into his untouched rice.

His father asks only one question: "Did anyone put you up to it?" and, when John answers, "No. It was my decision," his father nods and considers and says, looking right at him, "It's your decision. I respect that," even though his mother stands up from the table, knocking her chair to the linoleum with a plastic slap and stomps upstairs, crying "I won't have it. I won't." His father looks up at the ceiling where their bedroom is.

"She loves you, you know that," he says.

"I know that," says John.

"Okay," says his father. "Okay okay." They keep eating.

"It's a hard thing," he says. His father was half a year too young for Vietnam. Though they have never discussed it, John imagines his father would have done exactly what he did.

"I know," says John. "I've thought it through," although he hasn't.

"I'm proud of you," he says.

It surprises John how deeply he flushes with happiness. He feels his face get hot. He keeps eating.

The days before he leaves for boot camp are strange. There is the visit to the silent doctor. There is the fading of everything that is not his future—the halls in school, the grades on tests, even the popular girls and their burning eyes. He is already gone. He is surprised to find that suddenly he feels sorry not for himself but for the kids he is leaving behind—these young men and women in the halls, living only in their town, with only their small loves. They will know nothing of war, or of sacrifice. He allows himself for the first time to feel above it all, above even his old anxieties. There is another kid he knows of who is enlisting, a football player with a popular girlfriend, and in the last few months of school they nod at each other in the hall, tied together by the future. His friends treat him differently, make strange nervous jokes, apologize for talking about college, about moving to the city. John lives in the future and his present days are no longer his life—the mall too bright and slow motion; his parents kind and attentive and suddenly old. The news (which he begins to watch nightly) are a dream that he struggles to understand and no longer a channel to change—the green explosions on the night-vision camera feed, the angry bearded men raising rifles into the air. There is a certain pleasure in thinking about the tense uncertainty and likely violence of his future, his real life. He allows himself to imagine that maybe, just maybe, he will return home a hero.

He tacks an American flag on the wall of his room because he feels like he should and looks at it in the dark before sleep.

He takes to drinking protein shakes and running after school—miles and miles.

John finds himself arguing about the war with his brother, when his brother is home from the city. Not that deep inside he himself isn't ambivalent about the war, about the president, not that his brother doesn't know what he is talking about, but nevertheless John argues for the justice and meaning of the war fiercely and doesn't back down. It feels good to not back down, even when his brother says turning away, defeated, "I still don't want you to go."

The day of graduation several girls he does not really know insist on embracing him and telling him to be careful and to come home. He accepts each embrace with a ceremonial, manly "Thank you. I will." But with his arms around the girl he can feel her breasts pressing against him, and can't help thinking sadly: she is not mine.

His brother and his digital camera follow him around the aftermath of the ceremony capturing each person who shakes his hand or embraces him and each meaningless detail—the weak, wispy clouds, the empty bleachers, stray maroon balloons. His brother keeps nodding at him in a certain way. John thinks, as if we know each other.

At the graduation party that night at some kid's house on some New Hampshire lake he gets really drunk. He kisses a girl from his science class who tastes like wine and smells like the lake. Then he passes out shirtless on the floor.

When he awakes he expects to find his face covered in magic marker swirls, the word "RETARD" scrawled across his forehead as is rumored to happen at such parties, but when he looks in a mirror his face is clean, untouched, though his head and mouth feel painfully dry. He drinks warm water from the sink with the cup of his hand. He expects and wants another ceremony, some group breakfast, some goodbye, but the house is already nearly empty. He tiptoes out over sleeping faces and he sees what he is leaving and is sad, neither exactly determined nor resigned, but between. He has chosen his life.

Soon it is the time of last things: the last trip to the mall, the last pot roast, the last summer rainstorm. He stands at the screen door and stares out at their crummy backyard: the lawn too patchy to mow, bare earth and exposed roots, the new development visible through the sparse trees, a slowly deflating basketball that has been there since winter. The smell of his childhood is the smell of that rain, heavy and green and sweet, as if even their backyard is fertile. He feels very strongly he will never be home again.

The last Sunday he goes to church with his father and mother, at her request. He sits there and stares at the statue of Jesus in pain staring up through the roof to the sky. He listens hard, trying to understand or at least feel something, some rush of love for the church of the town, some sense of God to let him know he is on the right path, a good path, a meaningful path. He wants church to be important, but it just isn't. The priest's sermon is something about the devil and TV sitcoms. He watches the white flowers below the altar flicker like candles in the bare breeze from a tall rotating fan.

Then he is sitting at the airport Burger King, sipping coke through a straw while his mother cries.

He hasn't been on a plane since he was eight, when his parents took him and his brother to Disneyworld as an extravagant surprise Christmas gift. (What he had really wanted was more Legos.) He isn't prepared for the powerful gulping rush up into the air and through the clouds out toward the sun, into the lower limits of outer space. He isn't prepared for that exact ideal electric blue. The clouds below cover the malls and everyone who knew him, they cover the war and everyone who will know him. He is, suddenly, free.

Then he is on a school bus barreling through terrifyingly lush, non-Massachusetts-thick pine forests in the dark. The bus is full of other boys his age, most quiet. He is offered a cigarette which he does not accept by the cigarette-smelling kid in the seat next to him. The kid does not want to start a conversation, which is fine with John. He listens to deep, nervous voices behind him going on manfully about girls, about the war, saying nothing that assholes in his school wouldn't say, which disappoints him a little. Nevertheless, it is actually happening. He looks out at the forest and the empty weirdly unwinding road ahead of the bus and remembers marching in the Memorial Day parade as a boy scout. He remembers the white old houses in the center of town decked out with luxurious new flags, the winding gravel road through the cemetery, the old men in their uniforms and sashes, saluting. He remembers his terror at the ceremonial gunshots, the way they split the air. Some kid he knew stood in the hollow of silence their gunshots left, in the smoke from their guns, held up his gleaming gold trumpet and blew Taps. John sees that he is now more like those old men then that kid with the trumpet.

Then the bus is parked, the real soldier moving in rigid, measured steps toward the door to receive them.

He receives a pair of ugly, heavy-framed black glasses. He almost panics when he has to sit in the chair to let the unsmiling barber cut off all his black hair. He sits in the chair.

Boot camp is both more and less than he expected. For the first few days he is terrified of the screaming Drill Instructors, terrified even more that he will not make it. But he is never the worst, not in the run, not sit-ups, not pull-ups; not the worst at following orders or picking up the marching commands. Gradually he becomes more weary than afraid, those long marches in ill-fitting boots in the new wet thick heat, swarmed with mosquitoes, carrying the world on his back like a turtle and thinking like a turtle: just go.

He does not mind showering in order or keeping his bunk neat. He finds adhering to strict regulations satisfying. He does not fluster when the D.I. screams at him because of his improper buttons, but simply answers, accepts the push-ups punishment and gets back to attention. He watches himself with a certain amazement. He had his grand ideas about sacrifice, about gaining respect and honor, but he had always doubted he could cut it physically. It's others who fail. One pisses the bed regularly. The cocky one who talks about pussy every free second often screws up simple orders in drill, whines about his sunburn. Another can't bring himself to jump from an eight-foot high platform into water.

Although, at first, John keeps mostly to himself, he is surprised at how close he feels to the other recruits, almost like an older brother. He likes to listen to them bullshit. He hears in their boasting and banter a good humor and need-to-band-together-against-something that he has never before heard in the voices of boys because he has never before been one of them. He likes especially to listen to boys with southern accents. In their hour or so of free time before lights out he mainly writes letters or lays back on his bed and listens to the other recruits and nods or smirks at the right time, and is accepted.

The letters from his mother are all weepy affection and small town updates — the new traffic light by the hair salon, the fireworks. She writes about gazing at that stupid glass dolphin he bought her once for Christmas. He writes her spare news reports, "I'm doing okay. Soon we go on the rifle range." Amid the endless marching and cleaning and paperwork and eerie night fire watch shifts while the rest of the platoon snores and breathes deep, dreamless, he lets himself imagine his death. He will die, he knows, saving someone else's life. His father will be crushed but proud, his mother will weep, his brother will show pictures of him to his children. He imagines death like a hard punch in the chest or the neck and then a feeling like being a balloon cut from its string, a rising, a fading into the distance.

The bunk next to John belongs to a recruit named Buck, who John pegs as Mexican. John also pegs Buck as the one recruit least likely to make it through because he seems puffy and soft, nerdy. As if you're not nerdy, he has to remind himself.

Buck talks compulsively, even when speaking is forbidden. During inspection, while the D.I.'s back is turned, or even when he is just far away, Buck leans over and comments on anything to John—the weather, a baseball player the drill instructor resembles, the condition of the blisters on his feet. It isn't like he's testing the D.I. or being a smart-ass; it's like he can't stop talking. Buck is at least sometimes crafty, and measures his whispers, but he is caught again and again. He is caught bitching about the smell of the mud during the push-ups he is doing for commenting about how some other recruit couldn't even tie his shoes. Every punishment seems to roll off his back, even when the D.I. hollers everyone in the barracks into push-ups as punishment for Buck not being able to stop laughing at the recruit who farted during inspection.

"That's just the way it goes," he says later.

Everyone rags on Buck for that. Except John. Risking push-ups to keep a friend is worth it.

Then the first part is over. John and Buck are assigned a

rotation chopping vegetables in the kitchen of the chow hall for a nightly salad the size of a moon crater—so many vegetables, smooth and wet and endless. For John it is most satisfying to draw the knife through the strange sharp flesh of green peppers, over and over and over. He thinks about the millions of men in history who have given their lives as soldiers, and that he is ready to take their place among them.

But he also misses fiercely the sweet greasy pizza at that place run by Greeks in his hometown.

And he listens to Buck who fills every free second with his voice. Buck hopes to get a specialization in some sort of computer or communications work, which he can't go to college for because of money and because he can't not skip class. His plan for the war is to keep back from the real stuff, get out after and then get a job. He talks often about his dream job, the computer games he is going to design involving castles and wormholes and hip-hop stars with glocs. In addition to baseball, computer games are an inexhaustible subject: The night they crawl under barbed wire while the ground shakes with explosions and live fire streaks above reminds Buck of a certain part of a war game; the clunky, unpredictable M-16's they have to clean and clean and clean remind him of certain weapons in certain first-person shooters—he often jokes about finding the upgrades, the laser blaster, the flame-thrower attachment, hidden in secret compartments in the sand. John takes the rifle range much more seriously, putting his whole self into trigger control, concentrating on the procedure by hearing the words in his head like a prayer: Breathe, Relax, Aim, Stop, Squeeze. John tries not to imagine a person on the other side of the weapon, but he doesn't deny it either. He tells himself it will work itself out when the time comes.

Buck tells John one night, in confidence, in his lowest whisper, "I'll go over there, but I'm never going to shoot this gun at a person."

"Bullshit," says John in his new snapping soldier voice.

"I'm serious."

"Bullshit. And anyway, you'd get kicked out."

"If we get into it. I'll fire just a little bit up or down," says Buck.

"But then you'll just kill someone on the ricochet."

"I'm not going to kill anyone. I don't believe in it."

"You're crazy," John says. "You're a soldier."

"Turn me in then, if you care so much about it," says Buck with total confidence.

"Why did you join up in the first place?" presses John. "You could've just got a job."

"I want to see it, man. I don't want to be stuck in the same place my whole life. And then I'll get out and I'll be set. And don't worry, I can take care of myself. I'm not asking for your help."

Buck has a girlfriend who sends him letters every few days. Before he even opens the envelope he presses it into his nostrils and inhales.

Buck wanted a specialization in Operational Communications, John in Infantry. They are both assigned to Motor Transport. But it doesn't matter, John tells himself. They are soldiers. They are going to war.

John graduates as a coordinate in a moving grid of per-

fectly aligned, perfectly dressed young men. Even the assholes who only talk about pussy and guns are with him,
part of him, and not assholes, all the same, all honorable
whatever else is true, all soldiers. The brass band: metallic
yet warm and rich. He feels, in the best possible way, part
of a machine. But, when the ceremony is over, he is just a
little disappointed to discover he is still the same person.
The sky is gray. A slim redhead in a white flowered dress
avoids eye contact. He hasn't done anything yet.

After graduating, he has a few weeks at home before he
leaves for the war. He just wants the before to be over.
His mother puts on her brave face, her sad smile, especially when she is scrambling eggs, which she insists on,
for his breakfast. His father slips him twenties to go out
for burgers with his friends, although he never talks to
the boys his father thinks of as his friends anymore, and
back when they were hanging out they never went out for
burgers anyway. John hides the money his father slipped
him in the kitchen junk drawer. He goes to a punk rock
show in a basement club in Boston, senses people looking
at him because of his haircut, because of how straight
up he stands, against the wall but not leaning on it. His
brother comes home for a few days. They go together to
the sword store at the mall to buy a knife to take to the
war, a good one, and his brother insists on paying. They
share an awkward lunch at Chili's, talking about the Red
Sox, not saying much. The whole time his brother is home
he doesn't rip on him at all, not about his computer games
or about the girls in his class. One night his brother is
sprawled out on the couch watching some dating show

when John is turning in early. "Goodnight," his brother says seriously, standing up and offering his hand. "You'll be all right."

Mostly John runs, does push-ups and sit-ups, watches the news. He borrows his mother's car during the day for a break from her hair-touchings and offers of lunch to drive around the town and life he is leaving. He drives slowly, cautiously, more so than usual, as if driving around his town is dangerous. He feels a new tenderness toward his town: the mothers loading groceries into their sleek minivans at the grocery store; the random cows scattered across stone-walled in green and muddy fields; the crummy older convenience stores where everything is still price tagged with little orange stickers; the pretty girls at the mall with their cell phones and expensive shoes, that sliver of their backs between their shirts and jeans; the smell of ozone from the power lines and the first piles of burning leaves. His house and his town are no longer where he lives—they are what he has sworn to protect. He feels a new pride in himself, in his mission, so much so that he discovers that he loves the place he has always hated.

Finally, another airport, another Coke at the Burger King. Then, about to board the plane: his brother shaking his hand, again; his mother refusing to let herself go and instead standing there with her mouth closed and tears spilling out of her eyes. When John embraces her she loses it. Over and over he whispers to her: "I won't ride on helicopters, Mom," because that is what she is most afraid of, all those news reports of helicopters crashing, heavy black things being shot out of the sky, although

John knows he will, that he has no choice in the matter. He suspects she understands that as well. The exact last possible second, as his mother breaks her embrace, his father leans into his ear and whispers "I love you, son," not letting anyone but John hear.

Finally the plane in the air and out the window the beautiful deep blue of the upper atmosphere and below such distant green and brown patchwork order, the cities growing on the earth like moss on stone: so many lives down there. Again John feels pride — he is giving himself up to this great land — and at the same time a new feeling that does not fit of his own smallness next to the size of the land and the size of the war. He pushes that thought away and focuses on the shine of a river the length of a state, the shape of a vein in his arm. He wants to get over there. He wants his war to begin.

They have a few days to assemble at a base before shipping out. The first thing he sees upon arriving in camp is a group of soldiers playing touch football. One of the end zone markers is a flagpole. John half expects, half wishes for a Drill Sergeant to appear out of thin air and whip them into formation. The men grin and laugh and slap-five like college students on the quad.

They are welcomed and given orders to pick-up gear by a short, no-nonsense, spectacled officer, an unimpressive men just doing his job. A couple assholes ask stupid and unpunished questions about extra ammo. He is issued his gear, his pack, his helmet and flak-jacket, his gun that he might fire at an actual person, his chemical protection suit and gas mask that might actually save his life. A copy of the New Testament. He attaches his canteen and

ammunition and his new mall-bought knife to his belt
with duct tape.

Something about the base reminds him of Boy Scout
camp. John and Buck spend most of the days and nights
playing cards with whoever is around. John imagines
that purgatory, if it is real, is like this—warm days, green
grass and sunshine, ugly low buildings full of bunks, hot
bad food. The only women who are not fellow soldiers are
overly well-meaning local housewives passing out sandwiches in the room with the incongruous unplayed piano.
Daily, unimpressive men give unurgent orders about
sleeping or eating or make attempts at inspirational
speeches by saying things like "Remember the heroes at
Normandy. That's you. Remember the heroes in Baghdad.
That's you," and "Get ready to kick ass" to moderate
hooting in response. Overgrown uniformed boys, and a
few girls, sprawl out over every surface reading or cleaning guns or writing letters or playing cards or, mostly,
bullshitting.

It is as if there is no war at all but then, one fine
morning, the great journey. Lines and lines of over laden
soldiers climbing up the stairs onto a dull, fat plane built
to carry mail, or cargo; not people.

John and Buck sit next to each other, but neither want
to talk. Buck chomps gum and stares. John closes his eyes
but does not sleep.

The plane heaves trembling and thrumming into the
sky. There are no windows. It is like being inside a floating cavern, as if he has entered the mouth of a cave in his
old life, in America, and will only emerge after traveling

through the sky into the new light of the desert and the war as a warrior. He keeps his eyes closed and waits.

At what he imagines is a point exactly half-way across the Atlantic, Buck leans over and whispers into his ear, his mouth on his ear because of the noise: "You scared?" John opens his eyes and nods and Buck, satisfied, leans back and closes his eyes.

John imagines poking him and saying, right out loud, "Dude, I'm wicked fucking freaked out" in that overdone Boston accent Buck enjoys. But he can't quite make the thing into a joke.

It isn't until Buck asks that John lets himself truly acknowledge his fear. In that instant John is more afraid of the plane than the coming war. He can feel the weight of the plane and his fellow soldiers, the distance to the ocean below. It is astonishing that the damn thing is flying at all, that it is suspended in the air because of nothing but its unthinkable forward momentum. It is like being inside a whale. He has given himself up not only to the war or to America but to this machine. He feels suddenly that his story has already been written and finished. It is out of his hands.

He imagines a dark night in a tense, falsely-quiet desert city—the squat cement apartment buildings with arched doorways, the dead power lines cutting through the dark above, the shifting darkness, the dust on every surface and in his mouth and the angry men with guns waiting and watching behind each window. And there he is, following another soldier whose name he does not know through shadows of shadows, and there is a door marked with red letters. Somewhere inside that door down some secret tunnel, in some cabinet, in some luxurious bedroom dreaming about childhood and fruit, is the one they are searching so desperately for, the one whose capture could save lives and flip the whole war.

That door is John's door. He is the first man in. Behind that door is either the one, or a scrambling innocent family, or his death.

They have to stop over in a base in Germany. It is the first time he has ever been to the place where his family immigrated from back before the turn of the 20th century, the first time he has been to Europe, the first time he has been out of the country or anywhere at all. It is a gray foggy endless field of airplane hangers and runways.

The air base in Germany is not dissimilar to where they eventually end up: an airstrip on flat land in the middle of nowhere. However, the pavement in the war is hot, not only due to received heat from the sick, sticky yellow light of the sun but as if the pavement itself is a heat source. The dust in the air is particles of light. He is instantly soaked through and thirsty. The smell of sweat and oil. Scattered palm trees. Humming of hidden machinery. A labyrinth of fences, topped with rolls of barbed wire and concertina wire, the fences themselves surrounded by still-new ditches, keeping away the flat dull yellow-brown nothing in every direction. Inside the perimeter fence but sealed against the rest of camp by more twisted wire are missile batteries and black helicopters. The one road pressed into the dust, gravel strewn and driven over by tanks, leading from the main gate north, toward at the farthest horizon low green and gray mountains that are perhaps not real.

Soldiers everywhere, milling around in the heat with no urgency, as if out for a day at a beach with no ocean.

Buck has his sunglasses on before he even disembarks — these expensive purpley sci-fi things — and he grins into the heat.

They are taken to their new home — a city of tents set up on pavement that goes on forever. It reminds John of the parking lot of the mall.

They dump their packs and report to a mostly empty, marginally cooler airplane hanger-ish building where an officer, a thin, ramrod straight, terrifyingly clean shaven man, welcomes them in a few clipped words and tells them to do nothing, and to be ready.

After, they are given two white pills. An officer watches each man take the pills, swallow, and then inspects each mouth. They are told the pills will possibly protect them against a certain sort of biological attack.

Later that afternoon, they eat the plastic food from the brown plastic pouches, mix Kool-Aid with the chlorinated water. They play cards with strangers. Before long John's anxiety loses its edge; even the oppressive heat becomes quickly just another fact of life, an awful fact but everpresent, livable.

Before his first dawn there is the first of many chemical weapons attack alarms. John awakes before he awakes and throws on his gas mask and races frantically for a bunker, rapping his ankle on a tent frame, knocking into other scrambling soldiers in his mad hustle. But even so, when he gets to the bunker it is full. Some are standing at the door, pushing to get in, but John does not rush to join them. It is hopeless. They could never get the door shut anyway. He is about to die. He realizes he has no idea where Buck is. He is ashamed for forgetting about him. He scans the horizon and the sky for the incoming missile, the trace of bright smoke, but there is nothing, only the giant desert night.

He realizes, stupidly amazed, that he is cold. Barefoot, shirt and shorts, gas mask, that new rubber smell. There are other soldiers standing around the bunker and not pushing their way inside. So many intricate tattoos of eagles and flags and words and climbing vines made monstrous by the siren and the threat. In their gas masks and dangling dog tags, they seem half-insect. They aren't even trying to stay alive, only watching.

After the first night, whenever there's an alarm John makes a point of sticking with Buck through the chaos of scrambling men in the dark, whether they end up jammed inside the bunker or standing around outside it waiting wearily for death. Sometimes they lose each other. Each time John thinks: it would be so much easier if we held hands.

The work, when it comes, is a relief. It doesn't matter if it is important or not at first; it is something to do. He is trained as a driver, a part of a truck convoy that regularly carries food and water and weapons and supplies back and forth to another tent city base five or six hours along that featureless, barely-a-road road through the desert. Although Buck is assigned to one of the semi-trucks ("It's fucking impossible," he says. "The dashboard lights are dead and half the time I have to stand up on the pedal to get any pull."), John mostly drives a Humvee and keeps up the rear. He usually ferries around whoever is in command and his squawking radio. Although John does his best to avoid conversation, it is usually inevitable. The officer asks him perfunctory questions about his family, criticizes his driving as if there was any other way to drive before launching into some stupid story about shooting somebody in some other war. One at least has the decency to talk about baseball. John feels great relief when whichever officer finally gives up, sets his jaw and gazes grimly out at nothing. John takes up smoking simply to pass the time, to have something, however small, to look forward to every hour or so, to have something to do with his hands. He finds that smoking makes it easier to think.

Night after night he drives. The only break in the monotony is when the big semis sink in and have to be pulled free by the wrecker. There is nothing to look at but the immense blackness, the innumerable stars and the tiny dusty light cast forward by their convoy the size of a small-town parade that would have seemed so large and important in his town.

This goes on and on. He is always exhausted or hot or bored and trying to sleep or driving and thinking. The news of the war is neither wholly encouraging nor depressing—Americans die capturing and recapturing cities of dubious importance. There are rumors of chemical weapons attacks. He writes letters that say nothing about where he is and reads letters about where his life is not.

This is not what he wanted. Even Buck is frustrated. "I didn't sign up to cart shit around," he says, impatiently. "Maybe I'll just volunteer for the front. At least I won't be so fucking bored." Buck takes to hanging out with a bunch of guys from California who are just as loud as he is.

John takes to reading when he can. At first he goes through a few of Buck's well-thumbed sci-fi novels. Out of desperate boredom he picks up his government-issued New Testament.

He reads the gospels at first quickly, thinking he had read them before, although he hasn't really, only listened to fragments growing up when his mother insisted they go to church. It isn't specific passages he recognizes, not characters or stories, but something broader and vaguer, something about the tone, something about his reaction to the words, the way he doesn't fight the words or try to decode them as he usually would but lets them ring like a voice inside his head.

He barely processes what he reads so he reads it again. He thinks about going to church as a child, the young white-robed man kneeling and ringing golden bells and the priest holding a wafer of bread above his head (with two hands even though it wasn't heavy, John remembers thinking). He is amazed that he had actually believed in everything then: that after you died you lived in heaven with your family, that there was this nice bearded man who could make blind people see just by rubbing his spit on them. But it isn't that he believed in everything then, not exactly. Back then he didn't even have to believe in it or not believe in it; it was simply the way it was. He was as sure of God as he was of his mother. He remembers her face hovering above him, the smell of her powdery Sunday perfume. He remembers leaving the church on a bright winter morning, riding home in the back seat of the car through their town covered in clean, untouched snow. He remembers these things as if they had happened to some other person and taken place on some other planet, on Earth.

He can't remember when he had stopped feeling that way about his mother, about church. There was no one moment when everything changed but nevertheless, everything had changed. What did he believe in now? He wants to be able to answer himself and say "My country," or "Sacrifice," or even "Goodness," but he can't.

On the long night drives he stares into the night above the semi in front of him, as if for a sign, as if the answer will appear there in the form of a launched missile.

The nights he isn't out driving he lies on his bed awake, despite how weary he is, and listens to the voices of men in distant tents, so small in the immense windy not-silence of the desert. He sees how desperate he still is, and he also sees that he is at least not stuck in his old life, but on a search. He doesn't want to go home. He is a desert man now. He is a soldier.

John takes to reading any book he can get his hands on. He even borrows a book of poetry from the guy all the assholes call Shakespeare who is frequently crabbed up cross-legged on his bunk stabbing words into a notebook. He comes across this poem:

Batter my heart, three-personed God; for you
As yet but knock, breathe, shine, and seek to mend;
That I may rise and stand, o'erthrow me, and bend
Your force to break, blow, burn, and make me new.
I, like an usurped town, to another due,

Labor to admit you, but O, to no end;
Reason, your viceroy in me, me should defend,
But is captived, and proves weak or untrue.
Yet dearly I love you, and would be loved fain,
But am betrothed unto your enemy.
Divorce me, untie or break that knot again;
Take me to you, imprison me, for I,
Except you enthrall me, never shall be free,
Nor ever chaste, except you ravish me.

The poem is so strange—like a voice from another world in his head—but it is also familiar. It reminds him of emo lyrics, punk rock lyrics: batter, burn, imprison, enthrall: love is violent. He sees that the reason he loves emo and metal and hardcore and anything loud and whirling is the same reason he became a soldier and the same reason he is reading the New Testament over and over and, then, closing his eyes and joining his hands together and digging his nails into his skin and praying. He sees that he wants to be reborn as someone who is part of something larger than himself, and that he is pulled by this urge to violence. The only way to be reborn is to first be broken.

He feels his life which, he sees, even as a soldier, has been unfocused and confusing, funnel into a point.

Whenever he has a free second and is more or less alone he kneels and repeats the Our Father to himself, the only prayer he remembers, until his knees and back burn and the words become a hum in his head. After, he lies in his bunk buzzing, feeling close to something but not there yet, staring up through the canvas as if the canvas will tear and fall away and reveal the angel.

He feels like he is on the right track, that his life almost makes sense, that he almost believes in God.

He even goes to services. They are held in a tent among other tents, larger but otherwise no different, with gray, church-basement folding chairs lined up in uneven semi-circles. Some of the other soldiers carry black Bibles. The chaplain is a short man with thin wire glasses and a very rumpled uniform. He talks about how soldiers can do the work of the Lord, how a just war can be God's war. Something feels wrong. Still, afterwards, John forces himself to introduce himself to the chaplain, who smiles and says welcome and puts his hand on John's shoulder a little too close to his neck. John introduces himself to the soldier sitting next to him, a tall spindly pale kid with an enormous Adam's apple. They shake hands. The Adam's apple kid smiles a wide, complete, sincere smile and says "I am always glad to meet someone who loves Jesus Christ as much as I do."

"Yup," smiles John, nodding. "Yup. Yup."

Despite all this, he keeps at it. Then Buck catches him kneeling.

"Something wrong?" Buck asks warily, sitting down on the bunk across from him and putting the sunglasses up on his forehead. John doesn't know where Buck has come from. They have been spending less and less time together.

"No," John says quickly, trying to sit up nonchalantly, "Not at all." He couldn't stop staring at his feet.

"I just didn't know you were a pray-er, that's all," says Buck. A pause.

"Do you believe in God?" John asks.

"I don't know," Buck says. John forces himself to look up and Buck shrugs, leans back on the bed, crosses his ankles and puts his hands behind his head. "I mean my mom does, my family does. Or at least they go to church. I go to church when I'm home. It's what you do."

"But do you believe in God? Do you believe in heaven?"

"I guess I figure that all that will take care of itself and I've got to take care of my own. My girl and our kids, you know. The way my father took care of us." He sounds wistful, as if it's evening and they are old men, old friends, stretched out together on a cool sand dune at the Cape, listening to the sounds of the ocean. "I believe in something."

"But that's not enough, right?" says John rather boldly, hearing himself. "It can't be enough."

"My girl's enough," says Buck firmly, closing his eyes. "Thinking about going home to her, that's enough." And "I'll be home soon." A few seconds later: "I'll be home soon." No cockiness or zip in his voice. He says it like a repeated refrain from a psalm. Or as if he is reassuring a young child after a nightmare. Soon Buck is asleep.

One night, late, the only voices as incomprehensible as the murmurings of a brook amid the ever-present machine hum, John hears a saxophone, that sad ducky moan — this same descending melody over and over again with subtle pauses and variations like the call of a resigned, dying animal. But who could have smuggled a saxophone all the way from America? What plane or ship had it traveled on?

Just before leaving for another trip with the convoy, he closes his eyes and flips through the Bible randomly and when he opens his eyes his finger is touching this line: "But Jesus withdrew himself with his disciples to the sea." He recites the words to himself over and over as he drives, not only in his head but out loud, under his breath as low as the sound of the saxophone so even the officer will not hear. It is not a prayer. He knows he can't force himself to believe in God, to know God, to know his place. He can't force himself to believe in anything.

The convoy rumbles on through the dark. Ahead, the weak lights of the handful of semis and humvees and wreckers, his only companions on the face of the earth. Behind, nothing but the empty road erasing. The desert fits his imagination. He feels more alone than he has ever felt. But he is not alone.

An explosion. One of the semis in the middle of the convoy, incredible bursting flame even before the crack splits the world. John's immediate thought is "like it was hit with a missile." His second thought is of his friend, Buck, who is, he knows, in a semi closer to the front of the convoy. He somehow does not lose control of the Humvee. The officer next to him jerks to life—John hadn't realized the officer had fallen asleep. He also hadn't noticed that, along a strange horizon there were, just barely, a smudge of lights, a city, a village, something. How could they have taken a wrong turn on a road with no forks?

The officer has already shouldered his gun and is firing into the desert. Darkness moves in the darkness, closer. The radio squawks. A hail of bullets punches into the side of their humvee. Pinpoint fires in the desert burst and die; the darkness in the darkness moves towards them. There is no time. There is no escape. The officer's face is not whole.

John sees that the attack had come from behind, where he is, that the rest of the convoy, Buck, could escape. He sees this only after he has already yanked the wheel irreversibly toward the part of the darkness that moved. He is reaching for his gun when in the headlights he sees into the wild faces of men who mean to kill him. He sees into their mouths. He has no time to fire but ducks over into the dead officer's lap and there is a great ugly thud, he is metal and heavy and falling.

He awakes and does not awake in bed in a room, blurry but simple, as in a dream. There is a window.

He is in great pain. The pain is all there is, very nearly. He can't even imagine moving.

The face of a man in white with sharp green eyes that cut through even the pain bending down over him not in mere concern but in a sort of silent judgment.

From time to time other men and women come into the room and leave. He hears familiar voices.

He is able to distinguish day from night by the light in the window. The lights in the room go on and off in an incomprehensible pattern. At times they flicker.

When he is able to hold a thought, he knows what he has done. Whoever else he is, he turned and drove towards the fire. But he doesn't know who he has killed. He doesn't know where he is. He doesn't even know what happened to Buck.

He sees that even if he were rescued from this place in a flood of soldiers and cameras and carried by men and women whose lives he had saved into the belly of a great plane and so to America, home, he would still not be one of God's.

He feels totally helpless. He can't even make himself stay awake. Memories appear like random photographs sent from strangers: the smell of a summer rainstorm, his mother's face when she was young, the mall at Christmastime, the shore seen from the sky.

From time to time he makes out either distant small-arms fire or a burst of hard spattering rain against the window. The only other thing he can hear clearly is the call to prayer from the window. When he hears the voice he knows for sure he is awake, still alive. The nasal, needle-powerful voice is louder and louder each time, piercing into the hollow of his skull and filling it as if the call is his. He wants only to hear that voice. He knows he is dying and he knows that he has never loved anything as much as he loves that voice, as much as that voice loves God. He sees Buck. He sees his family and he sees strangers in the mall at Christmas. It was so simple and he had made it so hard. He listens to the voice and thinks, over and over, I have wasted my life. I loved you. I loved you. I'm sorry. I'm so sorry.

HENRY

AWAKENING

Henry David Thoreau awoke in the gray dawn light to a buzzing atop his chest. He opened the cell phone and held it in front of his face.

"Why is our door locked? Where are you?" said a young woman's voice. "I am standing on the lawn."

"There is a woman's voice in this object," said Henry.

"There is a woman on the lawn," said the voice. "There is a breeze in her skirt."

"The human voice is as water in a vacuum," said Henry.

"This is happening again, isn't it?" said the voice.

"I can hear a voice. The air has a voice. The air has a woman's voice."

BREAKFAST

Henry stood in the doorway to the kitchen watching the young woman take the carton of eggs from a transparent blue bag and then crack a few into a pale blue bowl.

"I don't think you have any more sick days," she said.

"You need to get off your ass and just go to work like everybody else."

"I am standing."

"What?"

"I am standing. I am standing before you."

"No shit."

"This is where I am. I am nowhere else."

The young woman twisted a fork through the eggs, tight-lipped.

"I sense a great change in the weather," said Henry.

THINKING

"There is a strange buzzing here," said Henry, sitting at the small white kitchen table, watching the young woman pick at her well-peppered eggs. "It is all around me and it is inside of me. The very molecules are a-hum."

"It's the refrigerator, Henry," said the young woman.

Henry did not respond but turned to watch through the window a few mostly bare branches shiver in the breeze. His hands fluttered from the table to his lap.

"The pockets of these trousers," he continued, "are not nearly large enough. And I have no sharp knife." His gaze settled on the basket of fruit in the center of the table. "I could never have imagined such large apples. I cannot imagine the richness of the loam in the orchard of their origin."

He appraised the young woman.

"I could never have imagined the skin a young woman is free to bare to the view of a stranger."

"Yes," said the young woman. "You are a stranger to me. We have never met."

"I cannot help but think of the white fuzz of the underside of a rabbit, just before the flesh is torn into by the butcher's tools. As all flesh must be torn into. Such must be the law of the earth; even this strange corner."

"That's pleasant."

He gazed downward, between his knees, into the linoleum.

"There is a pattern here. Lines the white of milk. Perfect squares."

He looked up.

"I should like to take a long walk," he said. "After breakfast. After I locate a bit of pencil and a notebook. And a knife."

EXCURSION

Henry was kneeling at the end of the yard. His khakis were already soaked through at the knees. In front of him was a large rotted tree limb that he had overturned.

"What on earth are you doing?" said the young woman. "We're going to be late."

He looked up quickly.

"I did not imagine I would be so soon discovered," he said, his mouth slightly open in surprise.

"You have been so soon discovered."

Henry appraised the young woman.

"The mist this morning clings to us," he said. "Already there is the moisture of the atmosphere in your hair." The young woman touched her hair. It was flat and stringy, as always. It was a little damp. Henry watched her touching her hair.

"I do sort of like you like this," she said.

"This is merely how I am" he said.

"What did you find in the dirt?"

"A worm, now vanished below. A few hard-backed beetles. And these few hollows into the earth here, and, here," he said, pointing. "Modest perhaps. But magnificent caves may open from keyholes."

TRAFFIC

"It is individuals that populate the world," said Henry, sitting in the passenger seat of the square gray car. "These cars about us are not a stream but a succession of separate souls, tending to the same flow by the confinement of a highway."

"Would you prefer we fly across town?" said the young woman in the driver's seat.

"It is no use to wish away gravity," he said. "Though one does wish it."

The window was open, though the air was cool and had a tang of smoke and metal.

"It is not like you to drive with the window open," continued Henry.

"I thought you didn't know who I was?"

"You are correct. I do not know who you are," he paused. The license plate of the car in front of them was outlined in neon purple. "I don't understand what is happening to the world."

"Right," said the young woman.

"We need to hurry the change," said Henry.

"A change of what?"

"What is needed first are days of unbroken contemplation. A plan. Then, assuming appropriate materials can be located amongst these pale warehouses, give me a hammer and a forest and a few bright days, and I can move the earth."

The young woman covered her mouth with her hand.

"Have I amused you?" said Henry.

"A hammer, yes!" said the young woman with her hand over her mouth. "Think of what you could do with a hammer! Imagine if you had a screwdriver! Or a socket wrench! Think of everything you would still not be able to fix!"

MID-MORNING

"What is it, Henry?" said the young woman's voice.

"Why do I find myself speaking into this object?"

"The phone."

"It is dark as coal and smooth as a stone from a swift moving creek."

"Is it heavy?" said the young woman's voice. Henry considered carefully.

"No," he said.

"What do you want, Henry?"

"I don't know how this object works," he said.

"The phone."

"The phone."

"You do know," said the young woman's voice. "You are using it."

Henry paused.

"Remarkable," he said.

"Henry, you need to go back to work."

"I remember a red dress. Against black windows."

"What red dress, Henry David Thoreau? When have you ever been to a prom?"

Henry paused.

"My love, I cannot open the silver doors."

"Press the button."

"The button?"

"The light. Touch the circle of light."

WORK

"I seem to be able to manipulate the images of numbers in a window," said Henry.

"I don't believe it," said the woman's voice on the phone.

"Neither would I, were a stranger to stop me on the street with such a proposal. I assure you, I can only speak the truth."

"Why does traveling in time make you lose your sense of sarcasm?"

"We are all travelers in time. Each of us. Every second."

"Get back to work, Henry."

"I would rather speak with you," said Henry.

"I wish you would say that when you were you," said the young woman's voice.

"I can be no other man," said Henry. "Do you see the two gray birds perched on the hanging span of wire?"

"No, Henry. You are where the birds are. I am over here."

"I often wonder if the idea of flight catches such a bird unawares. If they are surprised to find themselves suddenly in the air."

LUNCH

"It is as if I am addressing the universe," said Henry.

"It's just a cellphone, Henry" said the young woman's voice.

"I am sitting on a slab of stone observing the passers-by and I desired to share my observations and receive some in return."

"Is it at least your lunch break?"

"Ideas and sensations born in solitude and not shared do not exist."

"I see."

"You see what?"

"A voice does not see, Henry, if I am only a voice."

"But do not our eyes have ears? Do not our voices, our words, arouse sensations of texture, of cold and warmth, of the crisp snap of a bite into an apple?"

"Are you at least eating something?"

"Yes. An apple from my pocket."

"Is that all you wanted? To tell me about your apple? Can I go?"

"I was interested to hear what you could see."

"Well, Henry, I see a white wall and tiny traces of light on my eyes where I have been staring at it while we have been talking."

"Ah."

"Are you disappointed?"

"I only crave the truth."

"I see."

"You see what?"

"Just that. That's it."

"There must be more in the day," he said.

"Fine, Henry. I can also taste that there is too much lemon in my tea and I was just wishing I was ten years old again so I could ride in the backseat of a car on a trip to the ocean."

"I see a young man in a short brown jacket carrying parcels," said Henry. "I see a squirrel on the rim of a wire basket. There are strange long thin white clouds across the sky, like marks on paper."

AFTERNOON

"I do not like this place," said Henry.

"I know. I know," said the young woman's voice.

"The air is cold and I cannot feel it and my mind is overcome with buzzing. There are bees in the walls."

"One more hour and then I will be there to pick you up."

"I do not understand how or why I learned to manipulate these gleaming numbers."

"I know, Henry."

"Be it mean or cruel, we crave only reality."

"I know."

"The real cold. The swift cold of a stream, with tiny silver minnows like flashes of light pointing into the pull, and even the rich cold muck beneath, the bone and shell and twig and stone. The dead. The real."

"I know, Henry."

"This is not real. This is not my life."

"One hour, Henry. One hour."

LEAVING WORK

"I did not enjoy the time in that rectangular place," said Henry, nearly pressing his nose to the window as the square gray car backed out of the parking slot. "Yet there is a certain melancholy in watching the building begin to recede."

"You can be sad about anything," said the young woman.

"I am relived to hear a change in your voice," said Henry.

"I am sitting beside you and not on the phone. Put on your seatbelt."

"The light too has changed. There is a deeper darkness suggested in the hearts of the trees, a promise that the coming night will erase even these strange confinements. A heartening darkness. I could imagine driving into a sky pebbly with stars."

"You can drive? I thought you, Henry David Thoreau, had never even conceived of such an inhuman chariot as an automobile?"

Henry considered carefully.

"For an instant, I was somewhere else," he said.

The car screeched to a halt.

"Put on your damn seatbelt," said the young woman.

"I get sad sometimes and I get dreamy after work, too. But that doesn't mean I want to fly through the windshield because I forgot to put on my seatbelt."

Henry considered. Then he pulled the buckle out and clicked it tight across his lap.

HOME AGAIN

"Could this really be where I live?" said Henry.

"You were just here this morning," said the woman, slamming the door of the car and walking past Henry toward the small white house. The sunset was purple and orange just above the tips of the trees, and the earth was darker than the sky.

"I know somehow that I have been here in other seasons," he said.

The woman stood on the front step to the house, watching him watch her. The door behind her was a white frame. There was a breeze in her skirt.

"I do know you," said Henry.

AFTER SUPPER

"I sense a great change in the weather," said Henry. "I set out apple trees this morning."

"No, you didn't," said the young woman, standing in the door to the kitchen with a glass of water. "You were at work all day."

"What did I accomplish?"

"I'm tired, Henry. Haven't we done this enough?"

"I don't understand," said Henry. "If I was at work, what did I accomplish?"

"You tell me," she said. "You were there. You were awake."

"I have never met a man who was truly awake," said Henry. "How could I have looked him in the face?"

"Drink your tea, Henry."

Henry looked into the cooling cup of tea on the saucer on the table before him. He picked up the cup and sipped from it and set it down with a white clink. He looked up at the young woman, who looked down at the water she was swirling in the glass.

"There is goodness in this bitterness," he said.

"You know, Henry. At least I am not bored. At least when I am with you I am not bored."

APPROACHING SLEEP

"It is very dark now. I cannot see," said Henry.

"There is a little bit of light under the windowshade."

"I can see the light, but nothing in the room is therefore illuminated," said Henry.

"Hmm."

A few seconds of silence.

"Where do you imagine I will go when I fall asleep?" said Henry.

"Nowhere."

"Will I wake up?"

"You will wake up. Here. With me. But you will be yourself again."

"I do not wish to be only myself."

"That's the way it works."

"I will build a house in the woods."

"No, Henry, you won't."

A few seconds of silence.

"On a sidewalk in Cambridge, I saw a toad," said Henry. There was a catch in his voice. A few seconds of silence. When he began to speak again, his voice was clear and calm in the dark. "It had hopped out from under a fence the previous evening. The toad was frozen, quite hard, in a sitting posture. I carried it into Boston in my pocket, but could not thaw it to life."

"Did you put on the coffee?" asked the young woman.

"I did."

A few seconds of silence.

"I can hear myself breathing," said Henry.

THE CUSTOMER

I have been here all day, waiting to save you. I have been standing here all day at my register waiting for you as I scanned giant cans of soup, jugs of salad dressing, small strange kitchen appliances, packages of batteries, shrinkwrapped muffins and shrinkwrapped meat, DVDs, powerdrills on sale, shampoo, Tylenol, and, once, a trampoline. I waited for you while I counted change and thought about a slice of the ordered-but-never-picked-up white birthday cake in the break room. I have been waiting for you as I waited for the credit cards to come through, my fingers poised over the receipt machine, a chewed pen in my other hand. I have been waiting for you as I clicked on the light in the Seven so one of the managers would notice and come to give me ones and fives for a twenty or to okay the void or to retrieve a customer's desired ink cartridge or watch or thin gold chain from the cage.

I have been waiting here all day and I have been waiting here all of my life to save you, and I have not saved you.

I have not saved you, but I don't want to stop speaking, even though this is not my voice. I won't remember these words, although I will wake up suddenly in the middle of the night imagining that you were still awkwardly in my arms, that you were parting your lips to speak. I don't know where this voice is coming from. Perhaps I'm not a cashier, a thin young man with a scar on his forehead, perhaps I'm only a section of your brain that you've never before heard from. Perhaps what's really happening is that you're locked in your own head and my voice is just some captured but unconsidered fragment of your life cycling back on itself.

In any case, imagine what it means if these words are real.

I am not here to push you offshore with a final blast of poignant regret for the simple life you never appreciated. You understand—you have felt drunk with happiness when you were not drunk. I am not here to offer a final epiphany about the way people are fundamentally connected despite the accidents of money and body, despite what you thought of me when you first saw me in the corner of a glance when you walked into the store, how I was leaning sourly on the counter behind the register, thin as a thief, waiting for a receipt to print, my jeans dirty and low, my name tag crooked, my cheeks splotchy and pockmarked, my orange-blond hair sloppy and my goatee in contrast monstrously sharp and neat. I am not here merely to say that I am a person too, with hope and pain and breath, although these things are true. I am here to save you, and I have not saved you. But here you are.

Here is your life. Here is a photograph of your mother when she was young. Here is that city street. Here is a breath of his voice. Here is that painful sunlight. Here is the face beneath the earth. Here is a song. Here is the feeling of stepping in from the outside into a place like a hushed hollow in deep woods and here is the way you felt as the door closed behind you, the feeling that there was some necessary part of yourself that you could only sense here, in this place, in this particular light, in this particular not quite quiet. Here is the great question that you assumed would somehow answer itself.

Here is your worry. Here is who you were when I first saw you from a distance, coming toward my register with this look on your face — there was somewhere else you needed to be. You were wrapped up in a thick coat against the cold outside, carrying milk and a box of pills and a bottle of bright red cold medicine that wasn't for you. You aren't sick. Your eyes were clear, your head was up. You looked me right in the face and I looked you right in the face and even shook my head to warn you away but your attention had already impatiently shifted to the rack of candy next to the register — perhaps you were about to select something for yourself, or for the person who is sick, for someone you love. Perhaps you would have chosen a Hershey Bar, or Hershey's with Almonds, or perhaps Nutrageous; Butterfinger or Twix or Baby Ruth; Reese's Pieces, Reese's Sticks, Reese's Peanut Butter Cups, or Reese's Fast Break; Almond Joy or Mounds; Whatchama-calit; Skittles or Sour Skittles; Starburst or Tropical Fruit Starburst; Twizzlers in red or black; Breathmints; Vela-mints; Chicklets or Chunky; Three Muskateers or Milky Way or Milky Way Midnight; Five Fruit or Butter Rum or Wintergreen or Gummy Lifesavers; Orbit in Peppermint or Spearmint or Wintermint; Snickers or Snicker's Crunch or Nestle's Crunch; Bubble Yum or Bubble Yum Sugarless;

Fruit Stripe in Bubble Gum or Assorted Flavors; Mint or Cinammon or Mixed Fruit Mentos; Juicy Fruit or Double-mint or Big Red; 100 Grand; Dove Milk or Dove Dark; red or blue or green Breathstrips; Gummy Bears; Denteyne or Denteyne Ice; Icebreakers in Cinammon or Peppermint; Heath Bar or Rolos or Payday; Wonderball or Blow-Pops; Jolly Ranchers or Runts or Airheads; Laffy Taffy; Certs or Mini-certs or Smints; Tic-Tacs in Wintergreen or Cinam-mon or Orange or Lime; Skor; Kit-Kat or M and M's or Zero.

All of these are here whether you are here to see them or not in the same way that your not noticing the man with the wide-open eyes and the gun two aisles down did not make him disappear. You didn't hear the silence. You put your items on the belt and looked at the top row of mints. You were only paying attention to what should have been true.

I tried to warn you. I tried to whisper but you did not hear. I watched you looking at the mints. You were so absorbed. I hated you and I saw that I was the only one who could save you.

It all happened very fast and very very slowly. The man with the wide-open eyes fired twice in the chest of the cashier two aisles down (an older woman with stubborn red hair, you've seen her before) and you woke up into the world and threw your hands over your head and crouched as if to duck under the bullets that were already lodged in her body. You did not scream. The man with the wide-open eyes and the gun was blocked from your sight, you could only see the scuffed floor, the racks of candy and gum and mints above your head, my face. You could see a few empty shopping carts and through the glass doors out to the parking lot where people and cars were moving as if nothing was happening even though you could see that they themselves were charged with the piercing aura of existence — a silver car sleek as a weapon, a young man wearing an impossibly red sweatshirt. The specific is magnificent and murderous.

Here is my story:

I was seventeen. I tagged along to a party at an enormous white house in one of the new developments of enormous houses. The lawn was vast and treeless, the driveway was as smooth as a lake, the garage door could have held back a golden tank. I knew I didn't belong. I hated the house and I wanted to live there. When I got inside I kept my head down and went right through the crowd and music and girls to the kitchen and the alcohol. I slurped whiskey quickly, preparing the whole time to defend myself — but no one seemed to care.

I expected magic or at least danger, and what I discovered was kids who thought they were cool all packed together being loud and stupid. The whiskey gave me courage. I wandered around the party tipping over cups of coke onto the carpets, rearranging kitchen drawers, hiding toilet paper. I poured a beer on the back deck. I dipped a toothbrush in the toilet. I jammed a leather jacket underneath a white leather couch. I stole a fork.

I ended up sitting on the pink carpet of the upstairs hallway, listening to the blurry music and the slurred whooping coming up through the floor, staring into the flowery patterned wallpaper trying to make the 3-D dolphin appear. I was very drunk. The earth was tilting and righting itself with every breath. For lack of a better word, I was happy. I always knew I wasn't one of them, but in that hallway I didn't care anymore. I thought I had no part in their lives. It was all so ridiculous.

One of the hallway doors opened and a kid my age with broad shoulders came out backwards, carefully pulling the door shut. He turned and at first he seemed surprised and even nervous, but then he caught himself and grinned.

"You next?" he asked. His face was red.

"I'm next," I said, just to say something.

"She's out, dude. She's gone," he said, grinning.

And as I nodded and he ducked away down the stairs to where he didn't have to be alone, I understood.

I was drunk. I was happy and angry, and at that instant more curious than anything. I was seventeen and I had never touched a girl. I stood up and opened the door to the dark room and slipped in, closing the door behind me.

There was enough moonlight from a crack the curtains to see her on the bed. There she was. The last kid had bizarrely half-covered her nakedness with an open long black coat, as if to keep her warm. Still, she shivered in her mumbling sleep. She was gone. I knew who it was: the girl with the upturned nose and the short shiny dark hair. The beautiful girl. I could see her collarbone and the rise of her breast.

It was cold but the room smelled hot.

I can't say what I would have done next had another broad shouldered kid not drunkenly threw open the door a few seconds later and pushed me out into the hall. I didn't protest. I didn't raise an alarm. I went home.

I never told anyone.

I used to walk by that girl in the hallway at school and she didn't know me. She didn't have to drop out of school to have a child. She didn't send half of the party to prison. She went away to college. It was as if it had never happened, but I am not so naïve to think that she was not hurt, that I was not responsible. It happened. I often imagine that I saved her. That I wrapped her in the long black coat and carried her out through the light of the party into the safety of the night.

I think about her every day of my life. I know I will think about you every day of my life from now on, and I'll think earnestly about these two moments of my life in terms of the great questions that seemed so inappropriate when I was a teenager. I'll think about the way you can't help building your own soul, the way that, despite what you think you think, you know deep down who you really are, what you did, what it means. I leapt to throw my body between yours and the man with the wide-open eyes charging madly out of the store while firing his gun. For all the good I did, I may as well be a ghost. But now, I can see. I know that even if I had saved your life, I could never save myself. I know moonlight on the collarbone of the beautiful, helpless girl. I know the heat of spilled blood. I know what I could have killed, what I could have protected, what I held in my arms.

Are you still here?

Now it's summer. It's absurdly hot and humid outside and a Saturday so the air-conditioned store is packed with men and women and children seeking relief and socks. It's so hot outside the air-conditioning can only keep the air inside lukewarm at best. You've been at your register all afternoon, scanning and packing purchases for an endless line of customers. You try to look each person who goes through your line in the eyes. Memorizing all their faces would be too much, impossible, but you know that you remember more than you think you can remember and that someday, perhaps, if you were to see that one face in some other corner of the world, among strangers, you would not be alone. You are exhausted from the faces and the money and the work. You are hot and your head hurts and there is sweat dripping down from your armpits. The manager comes to your register and clicks off the light in the Seven and at first you are grateful for the fifteen coming minutes of rest but then he asks you to go out into the parking lot to help collect scattered shopping carts. You swear at him in your head. You finish what's left of your line. The last customer is a sour faced old woman buying four jumbo boxes of toothpaste. When you hand her the change she tells you to smile.

You secure your register and walk past the managers' station and the other aisles and push through the non-automatic door into the brilliant day. The heat and thick, hazy light radiate down from the sky and up from the pavement. You are burning. But, as you shield your eyes from the sun and look out over the chaos of the full parking lot, you can make out a black line of clouds just above the horizon in the west. There is wind. Already the clouds have moved closer. Men and women and children in the parking lot stop and point out the clouds to each other. You move through the waves of heat out to the end of the parking lot and pull a few shopping carts off of the strip of grass and jam them together. The small trees throughout the lot shudder in the wind. The clouds reach the sun. A hint of thunder, a drop of rain. Someone has flipped a shopping cart upside down so you lift it up and set it right and jam it into the others. The men and women and children in the parking lot are hurrying to get inside. A few are standing under the overhang, looking out at the sky. A flash of unearthly light. A snap of pure silence. The sky is black. A spattering of raindrops. You hear the manager calling out to you from underneath the overhang: "Hey! Hey! Get back in here!" He doesn't know your name. You pretend not to hear him. What can he do? The pale empty light fills the world suddenly and crashes and falls on you and all around you as bullets of water. You're soaked through already, feeling cooler with each breath. Your ears are ringing with the sound of the raindrops pinging off the shopping carts. The whirr of cars gliding by on the highway and the chatter of human voices are drifting away. A flash, and the light does not fade to reveal the ordinary parking lot but is instead becoming brighter and brighter. You stand there in the bright cool rain thinking only: let it come down.

THE POETRY UNIT

"A teenage girl is like a bomb," said Sister Helen as soon as I sat down. Her hands were laced together atop her unexpectedly bare desk. She was a tall thin woman in a pale blue suit with thick black glasses and a cloud of gray hair. Her thin lips were always cracked open, as if she listened by tasting the air. The bookcases in her office were full — not of Bibles, or three-ring binders, but of novels. There was Anna Karenina, there was To the Lighthouse, there was, unbelievably, On the Road. She was not what I imagined a nun to be.

"I'm sorry?" I said. It was the early morning of my first day at St. Luke's, my first day as a teacher. I'd been up all night going over my lesson plans.

"A teenage girl is like a bomb," she said. "I just want to do what I can to impress that fact upon you."

"I'm not sure I know what you mean," I said. I knew exactly what she meant. The halls were full of students, the boys in their forest green blazers, and the girls in their forest green skirts. The girls did not seem as young as I imagined they would seem.

Sr. Helen nodded, patient. She understood what I felt and she knew what I could not admit.

"Of course not," she said, unlacing her hands, opening them to me and then lacing them together again. I saw she took unconscious pleasure in her fingers. "I wanted to speak with you for your protection as much as theirs."

"Okay."

"It's really very simple. You are a young man, and some of our girls at times forget they are children."

"Right."

"Don't be alone. Keep your door open."

"Of course," I said, a little curtly. And she smiled.

"I have this first-day talk with every male teacher—I wouldn't be doing my job if I didn't. Our priority, before the life of the mind, must be the physical and spiritual safety of our children."

Thereafter if I happened to see Sister Helen in the hall I would prepare myself to give her a respectful nod, a "hello, Sister" (a word which always felt strange in my mouth) which she would receive with a half-smile and a somehow-sarcastic "Mis. Ter. Ship. Ley."

She knew every student's name. I'd never met anyone like her.

In fact, all of St. Luke's was alien to me. My high school was in the center of a small town, everyone in town went there, and barely half of the graduates went on to college. St. Luke's was off the Beltway on a hilly, wooded piece of land that was more like a college campus than a high school. It had a pool, and chapel that sort of looked like a castle that had been built just after the civil war. Students came from miles and miles away—some were driven more than an hour each way. Half of the teachers were former students. There was Mass every Wednesday morning. There were three different community service clubs and endless fundraisers, especially for one particular elementary school in the Philippines. Students were excused from class to attend pro-life marches.

A month into my first year there was an assassination attempt on the Pope. In the middle of my sophomore class the announcement went out over the P.A. After, I continued going over some homework about commas. Then, in the classroom across the hall, a television flipped on, and loud. I ducked my head out into the hall, to check, expecting a student in an empty classroom goofing off but there was Mrs. Dishington, the well-scarved Spanish teacher, one hand still on the TV and the other over her mouth. All down the hall, televisions flipping on. Class was over. We all spent the rest of the class watching updates from cable-TV anchors and the loop of a blurry, frantic crowd in Dublin, where he was visiting, and the helicopter shot of the front of the hospital. We watched all through the next class, even after word came out that everyone was fine.

I was not planning on staying at St. Luke's for any length of time. It was not home; it was experience on my resume so I could get a job at a city private school — hopefully smaller and more progressive — when we moved there after my fiancée finished law school.

It took me a few months, but I more or less figured the place out and how to seem to fit in. I learned, for one thing, that lesson plans were useless — halfway into whatever I thought I should talk about — representation of women in The Great Gatsby, say — I either found that I had no idea what I was talking about or that the questions the kids had were not the questions I thought they would have. So I relaxed and stopped staying up so late planning. The kids more or less did the readings and were more or less easy to talk with. I responded calmly to repeated emails from parents asking for updates on grades. I ate lunch in the faculty dining room and appropriately contributed my thoughts about traffic and the president. I almost felt like a teacher.

One day in late March, in my classroom, a senior named Josh Barsotti was hunched in on himself in his desk, his hair in his eyes. I sat in the desk next to him — I'd made sure to leave the classroom door open.

"Okay. Here we are," I said. I did not know what to say. I'd decided, stupidly, to insert a brief poetry-writing unit between The Great Gatsby and The Final Research Paper, and Josh had just handed in a sonnet — a not bad love sonnet — about a girl in his class. I had to convince him to not read it out loud the next day.

"A teenage girl is like a bomb," I said. "Do you know what I mean?"

"Not really," he said into his desk.

"No, I guess not," I said. "How can I explain?"

"I want to read it. I'm ready."

"Well, think of her for a minute, right? What is she going to feel?" The tips of his ears turned red.

"I just hope she likes it," he said. I'd never seen him so much as speak to her in class. Once, they were in the same small-group for a Hamlet project and his desk was pushed back from the group's circle. He'd held the book open not on his desk but in his lap.

"Find something else to share, Josh," I said. "That's my best advice."

Maybe I was getting a little too personal; maybe I was crossing a line a little bit. But he reminded me of me.

When I was his age the girl in English was Dawn Rybicki. It was public school, no uniforms, and it was a different time, like another country. The pretty girls dressed the same as the rest of us — giant T-shirts and flannels and ordinary non-skintight jeans. Spotting any sliver of bare skin was like spotting a tear in the world. She had this one Pearl Jam T-shirt — the white one with red circles that was only around before they got really popular — and she wore it mostly with some other shirt over it, even on warm days, but the shirt had a tiny rip she never bothered to sew up, in the seam under the armpit. It drove me crazy not to look.

Dawn was not in my social circle — her friends were the sort of kids who smoked cigarettes not just at parties but every morning on the way to school. She was not a homework-doer so she had not been in my classes, but she was smart and had things to say about books, even if she had not read them, so her junior year English teacher (the teacher everyone loved, the one who nudged me onto the path to teaching) angled her up into my senior Honors English class.

She would pin back her hair with tiny bright butterfly barrettes. One day she showed up to class with her hair dyed an incredible purple. I had seen other girls with purple hair, but her purple was a different purple. Somehow metallic, shiny, like it was always a little bit wet.

Of course I never talked to her. I wrote her letters, notes to be slipped into her locker that I never slipped into her locker. Even then, knowing deep inside that I would never actually send the letters, I could not bring myself to profess my love directly in those letters; I could never have done what Josh wanted to do. I wrote: you made a good point about Heathcliff in class today—don't listen to what Mrs. Peabody says. Or, I wish we lived in England. Or, if you ever want to talk about English, I would, too.

I can see looking back that it was lucky I never said anything. What would have happened is obvious now; it was always obvious. Our lives were opposite. I was in my room highlighting a novel for class, Pearl Jam on the tape deck, maybe the same song Dawn was listening to, but she was in the backseat of some older boy's car, screaming beautiful girls on either side of her, flying down highways, into the city. Or, even worse, she was in the front seat, alone with the boy, high, parked in the dark out by the power lines, his hand, his fingers under that Pearl Jam T-shirt, against her soft bare skin.

I saw her last year, home from grad school with Laura, my girlfriend who was about to become my fiancée. We went to the mall one afternoon—there's not much to do in my hometown but go to the mall—and there, behind the counter at Smoothie World, was Dawn—she didn't recognize me, and I didn't point her out to Laura. She was wearing the Smoothie World red apron, pulled tight, and she looked thin. She had a nose ring, and her face seemed drier, bonier, stretched out. She was still beautiful, but in a different way. Seeing her was deeply strange, like watching a character walk out of movie into the world. She was not connected with me in any real way. Feelings are not the world.

I'd met Laura, my girlfriend, now my fiancée, at a party in grad school. She was visiting her sister and already had a real job. We were introduced, and got to talking. We found that we could talk. What there is between us is real.

Josh's girl-in-English was named Stacey Webb. She was a field hockey player, and not even one of the better ones, as far as I could tell from never hearing her name on the morning announcement game recap, though she was one of the most enthusiastic. Her hair was always in braids, and she was freckled and, on game days, she striped her face with St. Luke's green. She often bounced into class, her boxers showing below her skirt, halfway through the chorus of some strange song. She had strong, smooth legs (I could not help myself noticing). She talked in class and did not, like her friends, complain. Characters had nicknames — during Gatsby, Nick Carraway was Nickels and Gatsby was Gatty. For those weeks she called everyone "old sport." I liked her.

I had become a little worried about her. At the start of the poetry unit she'd missed a few days out of the blue and had been strange in class since then. She started coming in late, just as I was about to get started, her books held tight against her chest, her eyes down, her braids the only thing that was the same.

She maybe had a broken heart — some dopey lacrosse

player, probably. Still, it was not only for Josh's sake that I tried to steer him away from sharing his love poem.

The first day I'd scheduled for sharing poems was an ordinary Tuesday, one of the first warm Spring days, new green poking out of the trees on the far side on the soccer fields, green that a dazed teenager could gaze out into, let his focus blur. One of those days you couldn't help but feel like you were a kid, too, and angry at the teacher for keeping you in class.

The kids filed in — Stacey as weirdly somber as ever, and Josh holding only a folded piece of paper, staring hard at his feet — it was obvious what he was planning.

I waited for everyone to settle.

"So we're going backwards through the alphabet," I announced.

"Mr. S, you are crazy," said Eddie Zymbrowski, the king of the class.

"Really I just wanted you to go first," I shot back. I was getting better at the back and forth, the tone, knowing which kids I could joke with, which kids would be terrified. (The idea of anyone being terrified of me I couldn't get over.)

"You should want me to go first," said Eddie. "My poem is the shit."

"Language," I said.

"You're the one who made us read Allen Ginsburg."

"He's in the textbook, right?"

"Not the poem you gave us."

"Are you ready, Mr. Zymbrowski?" I said.

"I was born ready," he said.

Eddie's poem was about the beach. Everyone at the beach had "a smile on their face." In his effort to add "concrete details," the subject of my last lesson, he listed flavors of ice cream, alphabetically, toppings on pizza, alphabetically and, in his poem's most memorable stanza, brands of sunglasses, alphabetically.

"Okay," I said after he was finished. "Comments? Anyone?"

"I like the beach, too," said Grace, one of Stacey's girls, eyes squirrel-bright. She had a wad of illegal gum way up in the corner of her mouth that she held up there when I was looking directly at her. Stacey, next to her, was slouched down in her seat, arms folded across her chest, pouting like a kid. I almost said something. Instead, to Grace:

"What part in particular caught your attention?"

"I don't know," she said. "The whole thing. It had a good flow."

"Okay. Thanks," I said. "Good. Anyone else?" One liked the part about the sunglasses because he could "relate" to it. Another volunteered that Eddie could put in the toppings for the ice cream.

"What else would we suggest that Eddie approach differently? What else could he explore?" I asked, finally. No one had anything else to say. As I glanced around the room the backs of hands and closed notebooks became too interesting to look away from.

"It's the beach," said Grace after awhile. "That's what the beach is like." She was right, of course. What could I say that I hadn't already said? I looked out the window—the beach was the beach—sunshine and sand and water. Ice cream.

Maybe if Josh wrote a poem about the beach, if I had, it would have been different—lines and lines passionate overdone description. There would be dark waves, fragments of shell, the taste of salt, a girl in the water, up to her knees, turned away, untouchable as a ghost.

As the next student began her poem—about a dream of riding a horse—I glanced at Josh. He had his absurd love poem on his desk. He was going to read it—I'd have to talk to him again after class. He caught my glance and immediately raised his hand, to ask to read next. I'd been right to start reverse-alphabetically—I ignored him; eventually, out of the corner of my eye, I saw him lower his hand.

After a slightly better discussion on the sleep-horse poem—St. Luke's students, apparently, often dream of horses—Josh again raised his hand, but I was ahead of him—I was already looking down at my class roster. I did not like what I saw there.

"Webb. Stacey—next in line," I said. Stacey didn't react at all. When students were sullen, or angry, or bitchy, they acted like they were ignoring you. But Stacey was a stone. "Stacey?" I said. Nothing. "Do you want to maybe wait until tomorrow?" I'd never offered such a thing. She stirred, but did not look up.

"No," she said into her desk, as if she was responding to some other question. After a few dead seconds she leaned over and dug into her bag and pulled out her notebook—St. Luke's forest green, sparkle stickers—and opened it in her lap and, without introduction or a glance at me or anyone else, in a voice quiet and weirdly firm in the bright, spring-dazed classroom, began to read:

> Be near me when my light is low,
> When the blood creeps, and the nerves prick
> And tingle; and the heart is sick,
> And all the wheels of Being slow.
> Be near me when the sensuous frame
> Is rack'd with pangs that conquer trust;
> And Time, a maniac scattering dust,
> And Life, a Fury slinging flame.
> Be near me when my faith is dry,
> And men the flies of latter spring,
> That lay their eggs, and sting and sing
> And weave their petty cells and die.
> Be near me when I fade away,
> To point the term of human strife,
> And on the low dark verge of life
> The twilight of eternal day.

There was a church-like hush. It was heartening, in a way, that the students would react that way, that even though they believed in the power of the beach-cliché, they could be stunned by something constructed so beautifully; they, too, were subject to the power of poetry. I was sure I was the only one who recognized the poem as the work of Alfred Lord Tennyson.

Stacey still did not look up — all the students' eyes were on her. I was helpless for words. Grace, next to her, watched her, then slipped her hand into Stacey's lap, and Stacey took it.

"Well," I said, in my best teacher voice.

"It was perfect," said Josh, and oddly loudly—the most words he'd said in class all year. They rang in the air. Stacey grabbed up her bag and notebook and was out the door. Josh had his hands flat on his desk and he looked out into the empty middle of the classroom, eyes burning, the corners of his mouth turned up just slightly. As if whatever was going on with her had something to do with him. Which was impossible.

"Why don't we leave it here for today," I said, even though we had five minutes. And, to Grace, "Would you? Check up?" and she gave me a weirdly chastened look, and nodded, and was up and the first one out the door.

I didn't know what to make of it. I puzzled over it the rest of the day, while I watched over some group-project planning, on the so-sunny-I-had-to-squint drive home. When I told the story to my fiancée later that night, in our apartment, her reaction was much stronger than I expected.

"What did her parents say?" she said. We were sitting on the couch with our legs tangled, pizza with paper towels, an exhibition baseball game on.

"What do you mean?" I said.

"You didn't call her parents?"

"Why would I call her parents?"

"A girl has a breakdown in your class and you don't do anything?"

"They're teenagers," I said. "Actually, she's eighteen."

"What does that have to do with anything?"

"I don't know."

"You just don't want to get involved."

"That's not it—I'll talk to her tomorrow. I have to find out if she knew she was cheating." She pulled her legs out from mine and sat up. She hadn't dripped the slightest drop of grease on her work clothes. She was amazing.

"Wait—she was cheating?" she said.

"The poem she read was by Tennyson."

"What poem?"

"From In Memoriam. 'Be near me when.' That one."

"I wrote a paper on him once," she said. "Back when I thought I wanted to be poet."

"Before you met me," I said. She gave me a half-serious eye-roll and turned away to a commercial for razor-blades. The tip of her nose was turned up slightly—it was the first thing I noticed about her at that party in that tiny, crowded apartment, all our shoes wet with snow. I was lucky I hadn't had too much time to stare at her and wonder before we were introduced. "I'll talk to her tomorrow. I'll figure out what to do," I said.

Stacey was in class the next day, more or less her normal self, if subdued, at least seeming to listen to Grace go on and on about who knows what. She'd tied up her braids with bright purple ribbons, for some reason, against the letter of the dress code, which allowed only white or St. Luke's green. Only some of the teachers cared about such violations.

Josh, already seated, watched her intensely, as if for a clue. It was not hard to see that he was nowhere in her mind.

That day poems went quickly—a rainy day at Grandma's funeral; a soul tormented in the dark; "memories that will never be forgotten." It was only because I happened to glance up at Josh and see the poem face down on his desk that remembered to halt class at the C's.

"Let's hold it here, shall we?" I said.

"Don't we have five minutes left?" said Grace.

"Yo!" barked one of the lacrosse boys.

"What?" said Grace, who liked to follow rules.

"It's quesadilla day," he said.

"Oh yeah," said Grace.

"Go ahead. Be first in line — it's really really important," I said, but they weren't listening. Stacey was not as eager as everyone else and only slowly pushed herself to her feet.

"Can I talk to you, Stacey?" I said into the hubbub, unnoticed. I had to say it louder to catch her attention. Her face when she looked to up me was like she'd been shocked, like she was about to cry. She sent a frightened glance to the door, but Grace and her girls were gone, chasing those quesadillas. I frowned in a teacherly way and nodded reassuringly. "Let's talk," I said.

I still had no idea what to say, and I had no idea what to make of her reaction. On one level, I wanted to simply praise her. After hearing all the poems, I could understand — why would anyone choose to read out loud a half-ass diary entry when you could read something as well-formed as Tennyson? Maybe she was the sort of teenager who understood such things, who understood that life was not the limit of your own brain. She was different than Josh, different than I was. She was mature enough to prefer Tennyson's words, though still young enough to steal them.

But she was not the sort to run out of class like she had after she'd read it. Something was going on with her.

"Everything's fine, Stacey," I said.

"It's okay. It's okay," she said, continuing some other conversation, still gathering her books. I watched her pick up her bag and then almost but not quite walk away. I sat down at the desk next to her. She did not sit down.

"Is there something you'd like to tell me?" I said.

"No," she said.

"You might want to tell me. It would be easier," I said. At this she sank into her chair, eyes on the open door, with great, weird longing. Out there only the same bustle of green-skirted girls and green-blazered boys passing back and forth, like they always did; it was like looking through a window into an aquarium. She wanted back in.

"Stacey?" I said.

"Can we close the door?" she said, and so quietly the hairs on the back of my neck prickled up. She had a lovely whisper. I did not know what to do.

"Why?" I said, whispered, then caught myself leaning forward. I pulled back. "It's important that we leave the door open—but I promise you have nothing to be afraid of." She watched the boys and girls walking back and forth in the hallway.

"I had an abortion," she said.

Some seconds went by and all at once she turned to me with alarm—I have no idea what my face was doing.

"What? What happens now?" she said.

"I just wanted to talk about the poem," I said.

"The poem?" she said. "The poem?" She folded her

arms hard and pulled them hard into her stomach and turned away.

What an idiot I was — and what on earth could I say to an 18 year old girl who'd had an abortion and was broken up about it? Neither of my college girlfriends ever had one — as far as I knew. And when I was in high school, all that I knew about abortions were rumors (even about Dawn Rybicki, which I did not let myself believe). In the cafeteria once there was a wild fight between a handful of girls about the origin and truth of one of these stories — there was screaming, and blood. And then suspensions. The word "abortion" had tremendous power which even I, an eighteen-year old virgin, a boy, could understand. And I went to a public school in a town where some people were poor, where people were used to making mistakes and getting by. In the St. Luke's lobby there was a giant framed photo of the pro-life club at the march, in matching St. Luke's-green ponchos, holding a banner in the rain, grinning like they won a race.

"There's nothing to be afraid of," I said for some reason.

"What do you mean?"

"You don't have to be afraid," I said.

"Are you going to tell everyone?"

"I only wanted to speak with you about the poem."

"What poem?" she said. She was clenching her teeth.

"The poem you read. Yesterday."

"Yeah."

"It was written by someone else. By Alfred Lord Tennyson."

"I don't know what you're talking about," she said. She was clenching her teeth so hard her skull was vibrating.

"It's a beautiful poem," I said, thinking. "It expresses a profound sense of longing." She turned a little more away from me, but still could not bring herself to simply stand and go without permission.

"Stacey," I said.

"I'm sorry Mr. Shipley, can I go? I really need to go," she said quickly. But then she caught herself. And she looked at me, really looked hard, waiting.

"You're free to do whatever you want," I said, which isn't exactly what I wanted to say. I should have said we should keep talking. I should have suggested a trip to the guidance counselor. But she was up and gone.

The last few classes were a bit of a daze. Luckily I had quizzes to give, so I could look out over the heads of my students, bent to their work, and think. I found myself noticing how shiny certain students' hair was, how certain boys had cowlicks, or wet spots where they'd tried to tamp the cowlicks down (standing in front of the mirror, handful of water, fingernails against their scalps). I'd done the same thing, in high school. They were so young. The sound of their pencils against the paper on the desks — a softer, richer more pleasant sound than when they used pens.

I thought about seeking Stacey out — but how would that go? A hand on her shoulder? What would it look like? Wasn't that exactly what I wasn't supposed to do? Should I just walk up and talk to the guidance counselor myself? Wasn't she a nun, too?

I couldn't possibly call her parents. But I knew I had to do something.

At the apartment, my fiancée was less conflicted.

"You have to call someone," she said. She hadn't even dropped her laptop bag.

"She's eighteen," I said.

"She's your student."

"She doesn't want anyone to know."

"You're not her friend, Daniel—you're the teacher."

"I don't want to hurt her," I said. At this she let her laptop bag slip to the floor, and she put both of her hands into her hair and sort of rubbed and pulled up on her scalp, tightening her skin—a habit of hers. It made her face look pinched, though I would never say so. But when she let her hands down her hair was mussed and she was herself again. She tugged her shirt out of her skirt.

"And I don't want you to be hurt," she said.

"Don't worry about me," I said.

"You need this job," she said. "We need this job."

"I'm not going to be fired."

"Really? You don't see anyone at that school having a problem with your conversation? With your little secret?"

She was always right.

"Call her parents," she said. "Or at least call the headmistress."

"No," I said.

I remember when I was like Josh and Dawn Rybicki worked at a record store. I had the idea to call with a question, a good question, a cool question—Do you have the new Helium 7-inch in? — and somehow she'd figure out who I was (I'd slip in a mention our school) and then the seed would be planted.

But I could not bring myself to call. I sat in my room and turned off all the lights and pressed in the numbers and hung up before it even rang. I pressed in the numbers and hung up over and over and over. I looked out my window into the darkness of the yard and hated myself.

Once my fiancée got into the shower I turned off the lights in the kitchen and sat there in the dark, with the phone. I called Sr. Helen and I told her. "You were correct to call me," she said.

My fiancée came down the stairs into the dark kitchen, wrapped in a towel, drying her hair with another.

"Why are you sitting in the dark?" she said, not angry anymore, drying her hair, her dark wet curls.

"I shouldn't have called," I said.

"You didn't really have a choice," she said, and she laid the wet towel on the back of a chair and touched my shoulder.

"I did what I had to," I said. "I did the wrong thing."

"Come to bed," she said. She rubbed her hand across the top of my shoulders. I looked up and could see her face in the dark and I reached up to touch the towel across her stomach, and under the towel to her warm damp skin, and to pull the towel open, there.

I didn't sleep much. In the morning I felt strange. My fiancée kissed me on the ear on the way out the door and my ear tingled. Standing in the kitchen alone I felt like my clothes — my new pants and the same old navy blazer, white shirt and St.Luke's-green tie (a Christmas gift from my sophomores) — fit me perfectly, like I was a model in a catalog. Driving in, I sipped my coffee from my silver traffic coffee mug and, at a light, I turned and another man in a suit was sipping his coffee from a silver mug, and we nodded at each other. The air was perfectly clear.

School was different.

The lobby was full of kids as it always was before school. It was too loud. I usually did not mind. A girl was wearing giant red sunglasses, against dress code, and her ipod was on so loud I could identify the song as one I had heard coming out of students' cars before, something about a bathtub full of cash — I almost asked her to take the sunglasses off.

I went right into Sr. Helen's office, not bothering to poke my head in first. She was halfway through dialing a number, but she glanced up and saw me and set her phone down. I was surprised to see that she hadn't slept much either.

On her desk, a yellow legal pad full of scribbled words. A Bible, closed. I was surprised to see that she'd been wrestling with something.

I expected her to say "hello," or "please sit down." She did not. I sat down.

"You seem upset," she said.

"What's going to happen to Stacey?" I said.

"Her parents have pulled her out of school," said Sr. Helen, slowly. I could not read her tone.

"I didn't know you were going to call her parents," I said.

"I am the headmistress of a Catholic school," she said. "I represent the connection between the students and their families and between the school and the community—my place is not to take the side of the individual student but to do what is best in the eyes of the Church."

I gathered myself. "Did you kick her out? Was that you?"

"I argued against it," she said, leaning forward just slightly. As angry as she could allow me to see. She took a breath through her nose and settled again. "But I can understand why a parent would react this way. A sort of cleaving."

"You knew what would happen."

"I suspected."

"She's only got a few months left," I said." She should be here with us." Us.

"That is my preference as well," she said, and then she sort of opened her hands. I had the sense that she'd let herself come unstuck. "And she still may return. There is time."

"Should I call her parents?"

"Not at this point," she said.

Stacey was of course not in class. There was a nervous feeling in the classroom, low voices. It was obvious that everyone knew (a late night text, words passed around in the parking lot, in the cafeteria). Grace, next to the empty chair, watched me out of the corners of her eyes — she knew everything.

And, Josh, right to his desk, his poem on his desk, his hands folded on his poem, his eyes on me.

What could I do but pretend nothing had changed?

"Okay, team, let's get back into it, shall we?" I said. They settled, as if someone other than I had asked them to be quiet at the same time. At Grace's feet, her backpack, covered in scribbled words, in pen. I wanted to read them; I would never read them. I looked down at my class roster.

"Grace," I said. "You're up." I found I was pointing at her with my two hands pressed together and index fingers out, like some ridiculous motivational speaker.

"My name comes next," said Josh, from the other side of the room and Grace, who had been obediently paging through her notebook, paused and looked up, stopped. I didn't look over at Josh.

"We'll get to you soon," I said, brightly enough.

"It's okay," said Grace.

"It is my turn," said Josh.

"Josh, maybe you'd like to wait until tomorrow?" I said.

"But I'm ready now," he said.

"Josh," I said. "She doesn't love you." I couldn't believe I said it out loud. No one moved, or breathed.

"It's my turn," he said, and stood. He held his poem before him and stared at it. Then his hands started to tremble and shake, so much so that the paper rattled. He couldn't do it.

"Try closing your eyes," I said. And, after a second, without looking up, he did. His face was red, but his hands relaxed and he folded his poem and lowered it to his side. After a few more seconds, without opening his eyes, he said "For Stacey," and began.

It was not the most original poem, but he remembered all of it, and everyone listened. After, silence. He slid down into his desk, and opened his eyes, looking up at me with a new directness. He was thinking: "Mr. Shipley. You don't know what love is."

I was proud of him; he would never win his girl; his girl was gone, but he read his poem. I was sorry for Stacey, that she was not with us. I wanted to tell my students that I wished what had happened had not happened, and that if I had it to do over again I would probably end up doing the same thing. But they would not understand. They looked up at me and waited for me to speak and I felt a tenderness for them that I knew I would never be able to properly express.

HUSH

When the phone rang I was asleep but rocking gently in the chair. Casey, our child, in my arms, didn't move. She didn't even seem to be breathing. Her eyes were closed, and she was warm.

The phone stopped ringing and a few seconds later my wife Kelly appeared at the door. Her eyes were mostly closed and her hair was a soft mess. Her nightgown was so new there was a crease across her stomach from where it had been folded in the Wal-Mart bag. The nightgown was pure white, and, in the first twilight of dawn filtering in from the parking lot, seemed to be floating just above her body. She came to me and unfolded Casey from my arms. "It's fucking Billy," she whispered. Then I was standing and Kelly had slipped into my place, already rocking, her eyes closed and Casey, in her arms, perfectly still.

We had only just moved into the apartment a few nights before, and our lives were still packed up and taped shut in boxes hulking like coffins in the shadows. Last night, when we got home from the last minute Wal-Mart trip for baby food, we were too tired to unpack anything. Not that we slept very much. The unfamiliar, just repainted hallway walls were white and clean in the first light. They reminded me of new money.

In our bedroom, the receiver of the phone was glowing green on Kelly's pillow, where her head had been. We hadn't ever given Billy the number. I hadn't even spoken to him for weeks.

But I wasn't surprised. Even though he had been cleaned-up for years. Even though he had been a Sheriff's Deputy since Christmas.

"What do you want?" I said.

"Mike listen we need you to come down here."

"What did you do?"

"Naw, Mike, listen. We're heading out to the State Forest off Longley. We're looking for a girl. We got a twelve-year old girl probably lost in those woods."

"Yeah."

"Look I don't have time," he said, curt.

"Hold up, I'll go. I mean of course."

"We're at the end of the stone wall in fifteen, all right? I wouldn't call but we need you. We need everyone we can dig up. Okay?"

"Yeah, okay, yeah," I said, but the line was dead.

In all the years of Billy's late night calls, I had never hung up on him. Not once.

"Fucking Billy," I said, out loud, too loud, but the walls in our new apartment are thick, and neither my wife or child murmured back. They were rocking deeper into sleep. My head was buzzing I was so tired. I could have closed my eyes there, sitting on the bed, and the rocking that was still in me would have carried me under. I would have woken up half-an-hour later, cold and tense, the carpet in my mouth. All at once I was scrambling to leave. I yanked on the only pants that weren't too expensive or packed away: an old pair of paint-splattered jeans that I would wear every day if I wasn't a grown-up. I was wearing a sweatshirt that Casey had spit up all over. I would have changed if there was anything to change into.

I can't say I was unhappy to leave. I thought about leaving a note for Kelly. I glanced in at the two of them. Kelly had pulled her hair back into a ponytail, like she used to do in college, late at night, when it was just the two of us. She had done it to keep her hair out of Casey's face. I didn't kiss them good-bye.

The dawn was weak and gray and damp. But it was good to be outside. I rolled down the windows and drove with the empty, shining streets, headlights off. I saw several signs for the Interstate with the names of distant cities. It was only after I was past the on-ramp, only unfamiliar stretches of familiar roads between me and the forest I knew by heart, that I thought at all about what the hell I was driving towards.

There was a girl lost in the woods. It wasn't hard to imagine. If you get pointed in the wrong direction in there you can walk eight miles without hitting a road or trail or anything. Small towns surround the forest and reservoir, but kids don't realize the difference between driving around it and going through it. And a kid her age could easily lose her bearings, get hysterical, turn herself around in spirals screwing deeper and deeper in. It's easy to lose it if you're alone. And it's not just the fact of being alone, even in the dark. It's how strangely not quiet the woods are, the way your sense of hearing becomes more sensitive. Every whisper of wind and rush of bird touches you.

When you are older it is not the same. When we were teenagers, Billy and I would go real deep into the forest, sometimes at night, but we weren't afraid. We had a purpose: to sneak cigarettes, to look at dirty magazines. Then, to drink our parents' liquor. Then he started going alone, with a girl. Once, a few years ago, he lent me a rifle and some bright orange pants and we took a few six-packs and sat very quietly with our backs against a giant rotting tree, waiting for deer that never came.

When Billy and I were younger we biked to the woods all the time, for no other reason than to explore.

The stone wall that follows the paved street for a few miles ends at the state forest/no trespassing sign and the old dirt road leading in. There's a locked bar across the road to keep out cars, but there's also a trampled path around the posts just smooth enough for bikes. It isn't much of a road — two tire ruts separated by a strip of soft green weeds. I have no idea why it's there at all. The road goes all the way to the reservoir and is intersected once by another, lesser road that on the one side heads out to the main street and on the other cuts into the largest part of the forest, growing fainter and fainter until it finally peters out about a mile in at a flat, vaguely circular clearing ringed with tiny bursts of white flowers.

What I remember most is the place where the two roads crossed. First of all, it's something to look down a road and know that it goes nowhere. Then there were the two slim trees right in the crux that were twisted painfully around each other. And more than that, in the summers, the forest would be teeming with loud insects, but the crossroads would always be empty, and cool, and strangely quiet. I used to imagine that spirits met there at night and waited near there during the day, invisible, watching. Billy felt them too, but he wasn't afraid. And he knew that I was.

The crossroads were about a mile in, and Billy and I would always race to get there. Usually, he would win, but on one particular hot, still, bright summer day, I was I keeping up and when the crossroads came up I went for it, I went crazy for it, and I had him. And when I won I threw my hands up and glanced around and Billy was turning off our road, pedaling hard away down the dead-end road, towards the clearing. He was just pissed that he lost, I thought, and that made me happy. It made me so happy. So I just kept going in the direction of the water, miles and miles away. My muscles burned but I felt the sun on my face and I felt at home. After a few minutes I turned and headed back to the crossroads, victorious. From a distance, I could see Billy's red bicycle, leaning on its kickstand in the center of the crossroads. Billy was nowhere. At first I pretended it didn't bother me. I called out for him. I knocked his bike over. There were no insects anywhere. The air was so hot and still it seemed to be itself the source of all the light. I heard something , but I saw nothing move. I found myself wondering which road led to the street, which to the reservoir, which disappeared. I started to cry. And only then did Billy appear, walking calmly from the road I had come from, a weird little grin on his face. He called me a baby and we fought until I stopped crying.

As I drove, my anger at Billy rose up in me, not for waking

me up so early that morning, and not for the years and years of waking me up in the middle of the night—but for leaving me alone in the forest. The streets were so empty the lulling of the wheels against the damp pavement and my memories of bicycles were pulling me backwards, into the old days, when it was just me and Billy and the forest, but when I rounded the curve toward the end of the stonewall the world exploded with life. There were police cars stacked up along the side of the road with sheriff's department cars, pick-ups with red lights stuck to their roofs, pick-ups without red lights, and one white van with the words "Morton's Housepainting" across the side. I parked my car, but left it running. It was the smallest car there.

There were thirty or so men and a handful of women, some in one sort of uniform or another, milling around where the dirt road began. They were checking their watches, wiping their glasses, tying their boots, looking hard into the dense woods. A few were drinking from Styrofoam cups. Their center was two cops who had a map spread across the hood of their car. The bar that closed the forest to cars was flung wide open, like an arm.

Before I had even taken off my seat-belt, Billy was standing next to my car. I didn't see where he had come from. His uniform was so new I could smell it. He was perfectly clean-shaven, and there wasn't a speck of dirt on him. He was grinning a little, that weird half-grin of his that wasn't jeering or friendly but uneasy, and a little sad.

"You almost missed us," he was saying.

"What am I doing here?"

"They'll explain."

"You tell me."

"Look, trust me. Let's go."

Of course I cut the engine and got out, leaving the window down. Billy was already heading back toward the group. He knew I would follow him.

"See there's a girl who we think's been in there since yesterday," he said, turned away. "We're just pulling it together now. You don't have to worry. Just stick with me."

"Fuck Billy," I said, and would have said more, but we were already standing with the group. Some were quiet but some were talking plainly, scratching their noses and looking up at the gray sky, as if it was any other day. One of the cops leaned into Billy's ear and whispered something and Billy laughed, a hard, manly bark of a laugh, and slapped the cop on his broad blue back. Billy was someone I didn't know. Then the cop with the map was talking.

Before I knew it I was standing just beyond the stone wall, forty meters to the right of a balding, off-duty cop in a white sweatshirt, and forty meters to the left of the dirt road where Billy was. Beyond him, only forest. The dirt road was the edge, the cop with the map had said, because their best information said that she was probably somewhere on this side of the forest, and, at least at first, they were going on the assumption that if she found the road, she would stay on it. Unless, I thought to myself, she had happened on the other road, and followed it, expecting to come out at a gas station, a paved street, and instead found herself in an empty dark clearing ringed with white flowers.

They had men with dogs already in, the cop with the map said. There were cars patrolling the street that traced the forest's edge. The search party, he said, is just one part of the larger plan. We were split into five-person units — in our group: two, Billy and the off-duty cop, to hold the flanks, two others, a uniformed deputy and a bearded man in workboots, to search the area randomly between the flanks, and one, me, to hold the center. The cop with the map was in charge of everything, but it was Billy who lined us up along the wall, told us to yell "Close up" or "Thin out" to keep the spacing, insisted to us that we weren't only looking for the girl, we were looking for any trace of her — any piece of clothing, any footprint, anything out of the ordinary. He said that he had once found a bubble gum wrapper that ended up leading searchers to a little boy. I hadn't heard the story before. I wanted to know where he had learned to be in charge of a search-and-rescue group, but, after he had set me in my place and took his place, he was looking straight ahead, then looking through me to the line of us, his face clenched and serious, his hand hovering near his gun. Billy was absolutely in control, like what I used to think grown-ups were like. The way they used to make you feel safe in the backseats of cars, no matter how fast they were driving.

Then, all at once, we were in the woods. And, since the search groups were staggered to prevent confusion, we were the first. It didn't seem like we were doing anything at all until we got a few hundred yards in and the street behind us vanished. The dawn gave up and a wet, vague darkness rose like mist from the heavy, pineneedled earth. The patches of sky above were the color of the underside of leaves, and the dull green all around moved slightly in a breeze I couldn't feel. The men on either side of me were walking calmly. Silence stuffed my ears. It was like we had been searching for the girl forever.

Billy was walking precisely in the center of the road, his boots hidden in the weeds. His paces were measured. Every fourth step he angled his head slightly to me, to check my position. At first, he seemed military in his demeanor and self-control — the uniform, the gun, the evenness of his motion — but there was something off. He walked straight and calm, but his head moved in little jerks from side to side.

Then I stepped on a dry branch and snapped it and Billy whirled to me, and met my eyes and let me hold him there too long. He wasn't in charge; he was holding himself together.

Billy turned back to the road. All at once that old fear rose in me. I was lost in the woods.

I had the sense that the girl was floating somewhere towards us.

I had to catch myself and remember that she wasn't some figure of my imagination, she was real. There were people in the world who knew her and loved her.

I tried to think of a girl her age who I knew, but there were none. I don't think I really knew any girls her age when I was younger either. They weren't really people to me — they were magical creatures living on some other plane of the world. The girl I remember most, although I don't know anything about the person she was, is one of Billy's old girlfriends. She had fire-orange curly hair, green eyes, and freckles in the hollows of her neck. I remember leaning on the hood of Billy's car one night, waiting for the two of them to come out of the convenience store, watching her through the window. She was waiting for Billy to finish scamming cigarettes, gazing past me to the parking lot and the dark street beyond, so calm, as if held up by the weird white light. She is still the most beautiful part of the world. I think that even now, even though I am older and wiser and know that the way I felt about her was due to my youth, my lack of experience, my cowardice. She was his last real girlfriend, and she loved him, really loved him, despite the way he was beginning to be. She laughed when she was with him with complete, ecstatic abandon, the way my wife laughed when we were with him, the days he was okay, before Casey.

The trees at the limit of my sight shimmered. I had a feeling that the girl was near, that if I put all of myself into my eyes, I would be able to see her. I was looking so hard into the forest ahead, leaping so far ahead of my eyes to the girl, that when sun briefly flashed through a weak place in the cloud I felt somewhere inside that I had found her. There she was. But there was nothing. It was the moment when the sun flashes over the apartment building next door straight into my eyes and there is brightness inside my sleep and I slowly wake and I am moving in the chair, gently, as if rocked by water, and Casey is heavy and warm suddenly in my arms. But there was nothing there. Then the flash of light evaporated and we were walking into the forest. Then I suddenly felt the crossroads, which I had not been looking for, and I felt eyes looking at me and I saw the two trees twisted together and then, like the light flashing, there was a deer, a buck, standing in the center of the crossroads, as still as if it had been there forever. I stopped quick and heard the sound of men all around me snapping out of their search. Billy, a few feet ahead of me, was already stopped and still, gun raised and held firmly in two hands, one eye squinting a bullet-line straight to those eyes. The buck's antlers were as pure and imposing as a church steeple. It would be a magnificent kill, even I could tell, I, who had never acted with passion on any living thing. The sun flashed. It was the moment when the light comes in the window and the water calms and Casey in Kelly's arms is heavy and warm and she has not moved. She has not yet taken a breath.

"Hush," I whispered to Billy, but too soft.

The buck seemed to hold the two of us in his eyes. Billy's face had not changed. His finger moved to the trigger.

Then, Billy fired.

The sound exploded from the center of my chest. Leaves in the trees became birds that exploded into the sky.

The buck turned before the thought of turning and ran, flew even, away from us into the forest, untouched. Billy stood there, holding the gun, still pointing it, as far as I could see, just slightly into the sky.

"Aw Billy, that's an easy shot," said the uniformed deputy near me. I realized suddenly that the deputy had drawn his gun and would have fired too in the next breath. Billy secured the gun into his holster, fast and rough and efficient. He put his hands on his hips and looked out toward the crossroads and the empty space the deer had left.

"Shit," he said out of the side of his mouth, to the men. "I can't shoot for shit." Then he turned to me just a fraction, that weird little grin creeping onto his face.

"That's a beautiful creature," he said through me. "That's something."

We stood there for a minute, almost looking at each other. I didn't know what to do, so I nodded, and he nodded.

I saw that when we found the girl it would be Billy who would approach her and hold her by the shoulders and look her in her eyes. It would be Billy who embraced her while the rest of us stood around the two of them in a half-circle, silent, not looking at each other. If we found the girl and she had passed from this life, it would be Billy who would go to her and kneel by her side and close her eyes with his thumb and middle finger.

I said: "Let's keep going."

THE
WILDFLOWERS
OF BALTIMORE

It is very late, the night before my seventh-grade son's science project is due at his summer science camp. I sit alone in the kitchen with the remnants from the process scattered across the table: the glue stick with missing cap; the new plastic scissors and the older, rusty pair we both prefer; bent and squished torn-out staples; dead Sharpies; a confetti of bits of plant life: fallen petals, peeled-off tiny leaves, snipped-off stems; shards of thick white card stock left over from cutting out the squares of paper (my son had insisted on perfect squares) that we'd used to write identification labels to glue on beneath the pressed and sleeved-in-plastic specimens: The Wildflowers of Baltimore.

These remnants would have been evidence of a missing child.

The finished product, a fold-open posterboard display, is impressive, especially and not only because he is a seventh grader; it is full of impeccably organized specific information, the product of hours of research and physical searching with eyes and fingers along the curbs and parks of our neighborhood. But I don't think it is exactly a true science project.

"Think about this: What is the experiment?" I'd asked my son when he'd first had the idea one night at dinner. He'd nibbled all five of his asparagus stalks in half. "An experiment begins with a question no one knows the answer to."

"Where do the flowers grow?" said my son.

"Well. Yes. That's a question. But the answer is obtainable by ordinary means. It's not quite an experiment."

"Can I find the flowers?" he'd said.

No one can win an argument with my son.

He did not do very well at Boy Scout camp, away in the woods, in the society of his peers. Science camp, during the day, is a better fit for him. Not perfect.

I love my son very much. What he wants from the world is not what I want from the world.

I find that I am also thinking of Otter Fisk.

I have loved the idea of being able to discover new truth through experiment ever since skeletal and croaky-voiced Mr. DeVrees, my seventh-grade science teacher, had explained Pasteur's experiment with glass vessels of broth that had helped to prove germ theory; he'd tapped with a fingernail his eerily neat chalkboard diagram of a glass vessel with a thin, swan-like neck and croaked, "Beautiful." My idea for my seventh grade science fair project came to me in a flash just after Mr. DeVrees announced the science fair. Morning light was making bright the black table. Across the table, in her assigned seat, Valerie Shammas. She'd just gotten her hair cut short and I could see the fuzz on the back of her neck glowing in the light.

I saw a question: "What liquid best helps plants grow?"

I felt instantly that my experiment would uncover some deep, previously unknown truth. Because of my experiment, grains would be planted and grown and harvested in the driest deserts, the murkiest swamplands, the stoniest foothills. The earth would change, my picture would be in the newspaper my father read, Valerie would hold my hand on the bus. I would ask her to be my partner and she would say yes.

But, next to me, Otter Fisk, rocking back and forth on the uneven-legged stool and gnawing on an already chewed-flat pen cap, leaned over and whispered to me, too loudly: "So what are we doing?"

Otter and I agreed to set aside the windowsills of our bedrooms for little cups of dirt seeded with beans. We agreed to pour various liquids—water, milk, detergent, beer, and Coke—over the seeds at regular intervals. Of course Otter did not keep to the schedule and his plants all died. But he apologized with his hand over his heart and meant it. And he wore a tie to school the day of the seventh-grade science fair and volunteered to tell Mr. DeVrees that I did all the work and then did, even though I said he didn't have to. That weekend he French-kissed Valerie Shammas in the basement at a birthday party I had of course not been invited to. I couldn't get mad at him, really. It wasn't like I had a chance with her.

A few weeks later, in gym class, I got hit in the face by a softball and cried, and Otter did not make fun of me but leaned in close to see and whispered "You can totally see the bruise already"; he was jealous.

Even though we were in different tracks in high school, we were sort of friends, mainly because he often started talking to me if we passed each other in the hall; sometimes he would even turn back the way he had come to walk with me to my class if I was antsy about being late, as I usually was. Otter was good at sports and friendly and not afraid, so he was popular, but he was never the prom king type, exactly. He was too unpredictable, too impulsive. Like the way he always sat at different cafeteria tables at lunch. The time he got in a fist fight with his own goalie in a soccer game our team was winning. The time in freshman biology he squeezed a test tube so hard it shattered and then had to go to the hospital for stitches.

Senior year I spent hours and hours in my room or at the library or in the classroom after school working on my science fair project. I taught myself calculus plotting software, I sketched out the structures of complex molecules, I looked up articles in obscure science journals that I could barely understand. My experiment was a derivation and comparison, via agarose-gel electrophoresis, of egg proteins characteristic of various local bird species. The day of the school science fair, the cafeteria was overtaken by fold out poster board displays. Otter skipped out of Auto Shop to see what I'd done, and then he stayed to wander the aisles among teachers and parents and the judges, obvious professionals making notes on clipboards. I saw down the aisle that Otter had stopped to talk to one judge, a tall bald man with glasses on his forehead and a name tag. Otter put his hand on the judge's shoulder and leaned in close and pointed down the aisle to me, obviously telling the judge that I should win. The judge listened, but tried to lean away, watching Otter like he was a beaker of sulphuric acid that had just begun to sing. When Otter was finished he slapped the judge on the shoulder and gave me a thumbs up as he went off to Auto Shop, or, more likely, to wander the halls until the next bell.

Valerie Shammas was wandering around the science fair, too, with a few of her friends, Art-class kids. I remember that she was wearing the frayed-rope bracelet she always wore. She paused at my project for a moment, leaned in, squinted to read the text because she only wore her glasses during class or, I imagined, when she was drawing; I was as close to her as I would ever be. I could see the familiar constellation of tiny moles along her jawline. "How can you know all this stuff?" she murmured without looking at me, and continued on, and I said nothing.

I won that science fair; I tacked the gold first place bow to the center of my closet door. I still have it somewhere. I believe it was winning the science fair that, together with my SATs and grades, got me that Trustees' Scholarship that let me go to college not only out of my small suburban town of white houses and football games on TV, but out of state, something that, I think, turned out to be necessary.

On impulse, I introduced myself to my freshman roommate as my middle name, and to my astonishment he believed me.

It turned out I was not who everyone, including myself, assumed I was: one of those bio majors who spent all night at the lab or the library, who signed up to help faculty with their projects in order to secure letters of recommendation for grad school.

Instead I was ordinarily irresponsible, and happy: vodka and Gatorade in mugs in cramped dark dorm rooms. I stopped writing bad poetry about girls I had never talked to. I met my future-wife playing Mario Kart—she knew all the cheats and once hooted with such abandon when she won that she was issued a written warning by the RA.

College went by. Life was full of days, not just ideas, not just plans.

I took a grant writing class to fill a writing requirement and did okay. The final paper got me the only internship I was offered junior summer. That got me a job, a good job that does not fill (or does not crowd out) my life the way the science fair experiment had.

Halfway through my first semester away at college, as I was just starting to understand who I was, Otter, who was in training to become a motorcycle mechanic, called late from somewhere with music so loud he had to scream when he asked if a spider was an insect. When I told him no and why, he screamed "I told you my boy would know" out into the noise and hung up without saying goodbye. I actually felt a little nauseous. It was like getting a phone call from an old life.

I didn't go back home until Thanksgiving. The town was eerily quiet. My childhood room was a museum exhibit. I ran into someone from math class at the video store—he showed me a new tattoo of a dragon swallowing its own tail and told me about a party that night. I'd never been to a high school party, but I was someone different now, so I decided to go.

A big white house all lit up like a prize in a gameshow. I went in. I felt not nervous or shy but, to tell the truth, superior. I had the weird feeling that what had changed was not my classmates, but me, my eyes. In the dining room, the popular kids were clustered around two seated red-faced boys gulping plastic cups of beer at the table, a drinking game. At one end of the table, a tower of empty Bud cans. One of the popular girls had noticeably gained weight. One of the football players had a wrist in a cast and a blotchy purple eye socket, like he'd been beaten up.

In the white-carpeted living room, Valerie Shammas was crammed into the corner of a long white couch along a white wall. She was wearing boxy black glasses I had never seen her wear before. She was shielded inside a black leather jacket that was much too big for her and scowling down at the arm of the couch; she had a lit cigarette in the fingers of her hand that she was resting her head on.

"You're going to set your hair on fire," I said, as if I had never before been nervous to speak to her. She looked up and regarded me without lifting her head from her hand.

"Why are you here?" she said. Not out of wonder or bitterness. A simple question.

"I don't know," I said. She turned away and took a drag

on her cigarette. I was ready to leave, but I continued on, deeper into the party.

Through the kitchen's sliding glass door, I spotted Otter out in the backyard shotgunning a beer with a few sweatshirted stoners. I figured I should say hello and then just leave but as I stepped outside onto the deck, Otter, for no reason I could see, snatched up a fresh beer from a torn open box and whipped it as hard as he could toward the bright white house and it thunked hard against the side and landed, burst and fizzing, on the lawn next to the deck. One of the stoners started laughing hysterically and another turned and put his hands on his head and said "What are you doing?" and Otter grabbed another fresh beer and hucked it at the house again, smashing through an upstairs window with a neat twinkling snap.

Otter spotted me then and grinned his loopy satisfied child's grin, the same as the day he showed up in seventh-grade science streaked all over with mud after a drizzly recess's touch-football game.

"Welcome back, Science Fair," he said.

Behind me, the sliding door screeched open and the girl whose house it was emerged. She had the same amazingly well brushed long blonde hair I'd noticed since elementary school, but now her face was twisted into the snarl of a much older woman.

"Otter what the fuck?" she said.

"Sorry," said Otter, shrugging, calm, the grin gone. The party spilled out onto the deck behind her. "I'm leaving anyway."

"That's right you are," she said. Otter turned to me.

"You wanna come along?" he said.

"I gotta go home soon," I said.

"Whatever," he said, jammed a few beers into his pockets and was off, around the side of the house.

When he was gone, I could not help feeling everyone's eyes on me, the old feeling, but then the girl with the long blonde hair, not ten feet away from me, started crying and mumbling about what her parents would do and someone rubbed her back and someone pounded on the sliding glass door to be let back into the party and someone clattered down the deck stairs to ask the stoners for a hit and no one was looking at me at all. I was not superior; I was no one. Otter was the only one who'd noticed my presence.

The newspaper said the police concluded that alcohol, marijuana and excessive speed were all factors in the accident, but I know it was not an accident, not exactly. And not a suicide, either. Otter simply wanted to drive fast and could not stop himself. He wanted at that moment to feel what it felt like to drive that fast. Like the way he wanted to feel like what it felt like to throw a beer at the big white house.

If I'd gone with him that night, he would not have driven so fast, at least. I would have asked him to slow down and he would have asked if I was afraid and I would have lied and said no, and he would have slowed down, and lived.

I didn't go to the funeral. I didn't want to think about it, then. He wasn't really my friend, I told my parents. He was just someone from growing up. I went back to college a day early.

When my wife shook me awake a few hours ago to tell me our son was gone, I was not shocked. Not exactly. It was more like something that I always knew would happen had happened. Somewhere deep inside, I knew my son was gone forever.

My wife left the bedroom to call the police and I pulled on a shirt and pants and shoes as fast as I could, though I felt slow, a robot. I went to look into his room for no reason. It was as neat as it always was. The bed was made. His closet was closed; the drawers of his dresser were closed. The bright fish hovered in the tank on the dresser. His desk chair was pushed into his desk. The desk itself was empty except for the display poster for his project, standing open. I saw the empty space right away: one specimen — the dandelion — had been torn out, along with its descriptive card.

"He's out looking for a new flower," I said to the empty space.

"What?" said my wife, hand over the receiver, on the phone in the dark hall.

"He never wanted a dandelion in the first place. I made him. I said it was a wildflower, same as all the other wild-flowers."

"What are you talking about?" she said, too loud. It was like we weren't speaking the same language. ("Ma'am? Ma'am," said the voice on the phone.) The hand holding the phone was trembling.

"I'll find him," I said, to try to reassure her. But inside I was not reassured. It was not the first time he'd disap-peared. His mind and heart worked in ways we could not understand, much less predict. Once, on a trip to the mall, he'd vanished from the restroom at the Food Court. We found him an awful half hour later, playing video games at Best Buy.

I managed, by gestures, to explain to my wife that she should stay home in case our son came back on his own and then I was down the stairs and out the door into the humid city night.

Baltimore was so different from the managed trees and careful lawns of the town I grew up in; it was so not empty; it was so full of other human lives and of the mystery of the world. But, earlier tonight, there was an unfamiliar malice in the city I loved: the brick rowhouses stretching in every direction to infinity, shadows pooling and shifting along the porches as I walked by.

I knew the only way to seek my son was to retrace the steps we'd taken, together, when we'd sought wildflowers.

My son was not around the corner at the patch of bare dirt between the curb and the sidewalk where we'd found his example of chicory. I knelt to touch what now-limp blue flowers were left. I could see in my mind each perfect square of handwritten description that he'd glued below each specimen. He'd copied the text directly from the Peterson Guide — he'd refused to see the logic of "using your own words." He'd also refused white-out; instead, if he made even the smallest error — a stray mark, a misspelling — he crumpled the offending square and began again. For chicory, along with scientific name and information about range and blooming season, he'd written, in his both neat and warped black handwriting, "The clear blue flowers that hug the nearly naked stems wilt and surrender their beauty by midday." I was struck by the simple fact: The flower existed. It was real. I knew the name. I was touching it. What if that is how my son feels about the world, all the time? Some things that seem small are really desperately important. Like, I want to play Half Life right now. I need to eat every one of these grapes. I do not want this dandelion.

How marvelous and draining it must be.

My son was not under the big sycamore where we'd pulled up the dandelion he did not want. (He'd written, "the hollow stem that oozes a milky juice when broken.")

It was so late that there was no traffic at all. I did not have to wait for the light to cross the street. I knew my son had waited for the walk sign, alone on the empty sidewalk next to the silent street. I felt for the first time that I was on the right path.

He was not at the little weedy one-unbroken-swing playground where we'd found the chickweed's "tiny, starlike blossoms" or on the grassy slope where we'd crawled on hands and knees, scouring the earth for the ideal example of white clover, "a pale triangular chevron on each leaf."

He was not in the gully where we'd found an explosion of the "golden-yellow rays" of black-eyed susans.

He was not behind the padlocked and graffiti-ed city parks department shed where we'd found a flower I did not recognize, blooms like tiny yellow-orange earrings dangling from the stems: the spotted touch-me-not, also known as jewelweed.

And then, there he was, further in, my son, without a

shirt, turned away from me, crouching beneath a big old beech scarred with a chaos of initials. He was tracing the dense mess of roots there with his fingers as if drawing a path on a map. He was alive.

I knelt and held him; his skin was hot and he did not stop tracing the roots with his fingers. This was the moment I first thought of Otter tonight. I saw him about to disappear around the corner of the white house, the last instant I saw him alive.

"Where are they?" said my son. He was not sad, or scared. He was angry.

"Where are what?" I said.

"The flowers that bloom in the dark. You said there are flowers that only bloom in the dark." I held my son tighter; I did not remember saying anything about flowers blooming in the dark, but I must have said something in passing. The idea had burned into him. "You lied to me," he said, finally giving up, his fingers hovering still above the roots.

"I didn't know you wanted to find them," I said. "We'll have to figure out to the right places to look. Or maybe we'll plant them ourselves. Okay?"

At home, my wife seized my son up and squeezed and shook him she was so overwhelmed and when she was done crying he said he wanted to go to sleep, but he did not object when she followed him to his bedroom and he let her sing him a song before he fell asleep, which he had not allowed in years. He asked for the Alphabet Song.

She's sleeping on his floor. She's wearing her sea-foam green bathrobe, a birthday gift from me that she had to exchange — three times — until she was happy with the color. I can see her in the Macy's, the bathrobe draped across her arm, looking hard at it, thinking hard about nothing but color.

At this moment it is all I can do to sit at the kitchen table with these remnants and think.

I've never been religious. My wife was — she went to a Catholic high school and was confirmed into the church, but she does not believe in God anymore. The first Christmas Eve after our marriage, before our son, late, I was awakened by the emptiness in our bed. I found my wife in the dark living room, watching midnight Mass on TV, crying. She said sometimes she wants so much to be able to believe in God again she thinks she does. But it never lasts.

I have also wanted many things very deeply.

I wanted to win the science fair. I wanted to ask a beautiful question and find a beautiful answer; I still want that, even now, my workdays spent proofreading copy and firing emails to other bureaucrats.

I wanted to know where my wife had gone that Christmas Eve. I wanted to find my son.

I want to go back and speak to Otter.

I remember what it felt like to love Valerie Shammas in seventh grade science class. For a few weeks after they French-kissed in the basement of the birthday party, Valerie and Otter were sort of a couple. She would every now and then across the bright black table pass him notes folded into perfect right triangles, his name in her purple swirly handwriting along the hypotenuse. How much I wanted to read the hidden words. How much I wanted those hidden words to be for me.

THE DAY

You have to abandon your car before you even get to the center of town. In the center of an intersection, a UPS truck tipped over, a smashed Jetta. Overhead as you run through, the traffic light blinks yellow to red, as it has for as long as you can remember.

You are already too late.

On one side of the street the old white Congregationalist church, doors thrown open. Men and women stand in the doorway, on the steps, facing in where you can't see. No one shoves to get in. They sing and hold each other; some have their arms wrapped around their children. You hate them. You are running faster than you can imagine.

There are lights on in the post office and the bank; there are lights on in the grocery store and its giant glass windows have been smashed. In the parking lot, a grey-haired woman sits on the roof of an SUV, cradling a bottle of dark wine in her lap; her head turns to you. Beyond her, from the grocery store, a man in a pale blue apron, the man from the deli-counter. He levels a gun and shoots the woman in the back of the head and brains and blood burst from her forehead and the gunshot cracks and you are not afraid because of the day and you think, "like a raindrop."

Then the man with the gun turns his body toward you and levels the gun and you jerk your body down, keep running somehow, your hands scraping the street, and the bullets punch into cars, whizz across the back of your neck, but you are still running. The man with the gun has turned toward the church. You hear the singing.

Past the gas station you turn and fly along an alley past a dumpster over a gully into the woods, the shortest route to the high-school soccer fields.

The orange pine needles make a smooth soft surface for running; above the are bare enough to see through to the whole of the sky, the day still an ordinary cloudy but bright fall day. No birdsong. You used to play in woods like these and come home with pitch on your hands.

You dig out your cell phone and press its face to your eye—no service, it reads, just as it has since even before the Vice-President cut into the Sportscenter repeat weeping, stuttering about Jesus. You whip the phone away.

Your wife, if she had left work the instant she'd heard and somehow navigated the city and the highway, would about now be arriving home to an empty house, a note.

You can see the end of the woods, the green space opening out ahead. You leap another gully and with bloody hands scramble up a bank of sandy dirt and weeds and there you are, at the edge of the soccer field, just to the side of one of the goals strung with tight insane neon orange netting. You stop for an instant to look out, to see. Not far from you two teenage girls are lying down tangled up in each other; neither is your daughter. Halfway across the field, the rest of the JV girls' soccer team sitting in a circle, some holding hands. And, there, in profile against the light of the day, your daughter. You can see where she drew her number, 14, on her cheek, in maroon, this morning. She does not notice you. Her eyes are open. Your daughter.

Love, a silver pin the length of the universe, through you; it is strong enough to hold the day here, forever, if only you can keep yourself from calling out her name. She will hear you and turn her head and you won't be able to see her face because, beyond her, the day will be too bright to look into, but she will see you, there, at the edge of the soccer field, reaching for her, too far away, blinded and full of light.

HAIRLINE
FRACTURE

Even in the moment when he lost control, Ben understood that for the other father to not merely place a phone call but to leave his work, wait in the turquoise carpeted waiting room for Ben, his wife and their injured daughter to emerge into the ordinary world, was commendable, showed respect for Ben's family and responsibility for his own child's actions, even though, as the school nurse had been quick to explain, there was no deliberate attempt to harm; it had been an accident, a game of freeze tag that drifted too close to the swing set.

Showing up at the hospital was exactly what Ben's father would have done.

And the other father's words themselves could not have been improved on: "I'm Liam's father. I'm very sorry. Is there anything I can do to help?"

His words were so serious and direct that even Ben's wife Mary Ann—who'd once gotten into a shouting match with a nursery school teacher who'd gently suggested that their daughter could stand more practice in waiting her turn—looked up at the other father with exhausted gratitude. She was holding their daughter across her lap, shushing her, although the pain killers had already kicked in and her eyes were almost closed. They were taking a moment to sit and breathe before worrying about the logistics of the car seat, the pharmacy. The cast around his daughter's ankle and foot was bright orange. Ben had found himself staring at his daughter's other, unharmed ankle — bare skin, because Mary Ann had removed that sock and shoe as well for some reason. Like a carrot, he'd thought, his daughter's blood and snot and tears still sticking his collar to his neck. He'd felt lightheaded. Then, suddenly, there was the other father looming over his injured daughter, apologizing to him. Before Mary Ann could say a word, Ben, "the calm one," snapped back, "Fuck you."

The other father, blank-faced, merely nodded. "I'm sorry," he said, and turned away, toward the doors out.

"Ben!" said Mary Ann, and, to the other father, "Thank you for coming." The other father half-turned, nodded again. His duty done. He was wearing a sleek black suit, his tie tight at the neck. Ben stood as if to chase the other father away and Mary Ann grabbed his wrist.

"Ben!" she said. Their daughter shifted, her mouth crumpling. Ben shook off his wife's hand and bent to his daughter and hauled her up roughly from his wife's lap.

"What?" he said, too loud, his daughter squirming, burrowing into his neck, like an animal. She was somehow heavier than he expected; she never wanted to be carried anymore. Her skin was hot and she choked back a breath, which meant she was about to cry. Ben's wife stood, opened her arms.

"Give her back," she said. "You're scaring her."

Ben did not respond or give her back but allowed his wife to collect his daughter from him. Immediately she calmed, hitched herself up on her mother's hip, turned her head to lay it across her mother's shoulder to look back at him with wet black eyes. Her bright orange cast hung awkwardly across his wife's stomach; her toes were bright red. His wife struggled to support all of the weight and tried to keep their daughter's injured leg still with outstretched, trembling fingers. He felt like his hands were swelling. His wife laid her other hand across their daughter's forehead, as if to shield her from him.

"What was I supposed to say?" he said, too loud, hearing himself but unable to stop himself.

"It doesn't matter right now," she said and turned away as if, Ben felt, to turn her back to him, but she was only gathering her bag. She half dipped her body, nearly tipping over, and Ben did not move to help. "Why don't you just head back to work?" she said when she'd righted herself.

"I'm not going back to work," he said.

"I can't deal with you like this. Whatever you've turned into. It's not helpful."

"What do you mean what I've turned into?" he said.

"Nothing. Ben."

"What do you mean I'm not helpful?"

"I'm sorry. You're right. Look—you got to her first. You brought her here. Let me take her home. Let me take care of her."

"I'm not going back to work."

"I don't care, Ben. But she needs some quiet."

"Fine," he said. He watched his wife's fingers smooth his daughter's hair back from her forehead. His wife, watching him to see what he would do next, was a stranger.

"I'll carry her out to your car," said Ben, finally, and moved in to take his daughter back although she clung, at first, to her mother, and then to a few strands of her mother's hair that her mother eased from her fingers as she squirmed and scraped her forehead against the day's beard under his jaw and choked a breath and almost started to cry but Ben whispered "It's okay. It's okay," and turned and walked to the doors and out into the windy clear bright day, and she whimpered and shifted and was quiet in his arms.

A few minutes later he found himself behind the wheel of his car at the hospital exit, foot on the brake, no idea in his head of where to go. He should just head back to the office: there was much to be done, as there always was. There was that programming meeting he could be sitting in on, the grant application to finish.

He could see his office: the new mesh-backed black office chair he did not just like but, in truth, loved, the way it held him firmly but softly. The plain white walls bare but for a framed "Great Artists: Cezanne" print, a blurry and boxy but magically lush green mountain, that had been in the office when he'd moved in. The image had become his, part of his imagination and even his dreams. In the same way he could close his eyes and see the view out of his window: a corner of the office building opposite — brick and black windows. Parking lot, saplings in boxes. Sky.

He could hear the chime of the computer as he tapped a key and the monitor bloomed awake to show him his little garden of tasks.

He belonged there. But the office would not collapse without him, he thought. It should collapse without him. He saw the photographs of his wife and daughter in their thin chrome frames on the corner of his desk, half obscured by wire trays full of stacked undone paperwork.

He began to unbutton his stained and sticky work shirt to take it off and it was only the grumble of a UPS truck behind him that brought him back into the car. He tore his work shirt off and tossed it into the empty seat behind him and pulled out without thinking — not left, toward work and, past work, home, but right, toward the city.

He tugged loose the collar of his white T-shirt as he drove — it was stained as well, at the neck (he saw in the tipped down rearview mirror), but less so. It was somehow like the patch of water damage on the ceiling of their extra, empty bedroom.

He would not have imagined that his daughter's injury could have affected him so much; she would be fine; she would heal. After all, he'd healed. When he had broken his wrist as a child, leaping for a tossed football in the backyard, he hadn't even thought to cry, the sensation was so strange, a twisted, impossible squeezing. And when he came upon his mother in the kitchen he'd felt more ashamed than scared, especially because of the way she'd knelt and let her hand hover beneath his hand that cradled his broken wrist, the way she sighed and said "Oh, Benjamin."

Aside from the horrible pain of the doctor's examination (through which he'd bitten his cheek to keep from crying) — the time at the hospital had been more interesting than anything else — the heavy lead apron, the moments left alone in the x-ray room while the dark machine whirred, the fog of the painkillers floating him inside himself and giving the edges of things a buzzing soft light. He could still feel the odd heavy rough wet of the casting material being wrapped around his skin; he could still feel the cast hardening around his wrist. His pink alien fingers.

His father had stood by the doorway in his Saturday clothes — work jeans and grimy fingers — asking clipped questions of the doctors, watching carefully.

"It's only a hairline fracture," he'd said, his hand for a moment on his Ben's shoulder, as they walked to the car, as if Ben had not himself heard the doctor.

When his wife had called him with the news that morning she could barely speak she was so upset and out of breath, both because of the injury itself and because she was so far away, all the way down in DC for the morning to meet up with a college roommate. Ben had listened and understood immediately and responded: "Calm down. I'm only ten minutes away from school. I'm leaving now." And he'd heard, not for the first time, his father's voice in his own.

And when he hung up the phone he felt not frantic but calm, his father's calm that came from focusing on simply doing what needed to be done. He composed a quick email to his boss, read it through twice, and sent it. He saved his work on the grant application and logged off his account before standing. He did not collect his jacket from the back of the door — not because he forgot but because the day would be warm enough, he reasoned — it was almost April, and the sun was supposed to break through before noon. Besides, he'd be back before long.

He walked quickly to his car.

He drove to the school as far above the speed limit as was reasonable.

He parked in a visitor spot in the school parking lot, not in front, because of the big yellow "no parking" painted on the curb there. He locked the doors of his car and walked quickly into the school and waited his turn at the main office behind a UPS delivery woman in shorts, who was getting a signature for a box from Office Depot.

The secretary in the office reacted with widened eyes when he gave his name. "Sorry," she said, as if there was something she had to apologize for. "I didn't know it was you. This way." She came swiftly around the desk, deliberately gesturing the way forward with an opened hand and Ben followed behind into the hall, his calm leaking away even before he heard, through the closed door with a small turquoise plaque that read "Nurse," his daughter. She was not crying exactly but that sort of grunting and whimpering, in waves, that meant she was trying to stop crying but could not.

Ben was obscurely grateful to the secretary for not leaving him alone before the door but turning the door-knob and entering first. "Here's the father," she said, and stepped out of the way, her hand remaining on the door-knob, and he stepped in and saw the nurse not merely bending over his daughter but sitting with her on the bright white bed, the nurse with her pearl earrings and graying hair and wrinkled mouth awkwardly cradling his daughter. He could see that his daughter's half-turned away face was streaked with tears and snot and even blood—she often got bloody noses when her nose was running. She'd lost the sparkly blue headband her mother had insisted she put on not four hours before.

Ben took two steps in and stopped and did not know what to do and said "Thank you," to no one, and then his daughter heard his voice and twisted her head and rolled her eyes to see him, and screamed.

Ben drove away from the hospital past a gas station, a golf course, and the Welcome to Baltimore sign, just beyond which was a cross street that would shoot him West to the highway and then the Beltway and work or home. He did not turn. Soon enough he was idling at a red light next to a few boarded up rowhouses—one with black burns smearing up from the upper windows. The brick of the rowhouses was a rich soft red and powdery, as if sandpapered by years and years of wind.

On the other side of the street, a bus stop, a bench with several wooden slats torn up from its seat. Even though it was only just spring, bright weedy grass was already poking up through cracks in the sidewalk. He hadn't lived in a place with sidewalks for years. A young man, face shadowed inside the hood of his sweatshirt, was perched on the back of the bench. Giant white untied shoes. Ben didn't realize he was staring until the young man shifted his head down and knocked the hood back from his face and leaned forward and was about to say something but the light was green and Ben was moving again. He shivered and took the next right for no reason.

Soon he was driving into the neighborhood around the university. Tall apartment buildings lined by architectural scrollwork. Black iron fencing. The grass in the lane divider had recently been mowed — someone had had to drag a lawnmower across the street, Ben saw. The sidewalks were smooth; here and there a student or a knot of students coming from or heading to class with black or gray shoulder bags or intricately strapped backpacks, touchscreen phones they stared down into as they walked. There was something so professional about college kids these days, Ben thought. He did not recognize his uncertain younger self anywhere.

The first time he'd seen Mary Ann at college he'd been throwing a baseball back and forth down a dorm hallway and almost hit her — she'd emerged from an open door just as he released the ball; she'd spotted it and dipped her head in the same instant.

"Nice reflexes," he'd said; he was usually too shy to say anything at all to people he didn't know but the whole thing had happened so fast that his observation, the note of honest appreciation, flew out of his mouth before he had even seen how pretty she was, her dark eyes and dark hair. He'd been lucky. The ice was broken, an achievement, even though he'd almost hurt her, even though in the moment she didn't turn and respond to him but ducked into another room and closed the door behind her.

They met again a few nights later, crammed into someone else's dorm room, vodka and Gatorade in Star

Wars cups. The lights were off but he could still see her profile against the weak light from the window that looked out over a parking lot. No one had ever been so beautiful; after he apologized for almost hitting her with the baseball she smiled in the dark, as if at a private joke and Ben somehow did not let it go but pressed on, asked,

"What's funny?"

"It's just that was the most intense apology I've ever gotten," she said.

"There's more where that came from," he said, thinking, what are you saying? But she laughed. And anything was possible.

Ben, driving, told himself the college kids only seem like grown up robots because you didn't have a phone like that when you were their age. They are still kids; they get drunk and fall in love in dorm hallways just like you did. You just can't see that part of their lives; you can't see into their heads. You're just you.

He drove past the statue of the lacrosse player frozen in turbulent bronze motion outside the Lacrosse Hall of Fame, then a parking garage, then the church of Christian Science that looked like a Greek temple from a textbook but was somehow a real place. What on earth would it be like to be a Christian Scientist? Ben thought. On the sidewalk, a woman younger than Mary Ann was pushing a toddler in a bright red stroller, the same stroller they'd used when their daughter was that age, a complicated tiny spaceship that Ben always had trouble folding up. Once he'd pinched the soft web of skin between his thumb and index finger in a hinge, wiped the blood on his forehead before he realized he was bleeding.

He touched his forehead and it was clammy with dried sweat.

To go straight would take him toward the highway past that French restaurant he'd been to a few times with Mary Ann. She'd had to remind him ahead of time not to complain about the thirteen dollar salad. When they went to the trouble of paying for a sitter to have a night out, she liked to shower just before. The smell of her just washed hair. Ben took the left, deeper into the city.

More rowhouses — these with freshly painted columns, already thick blankets of grass in front, just-starting-to-flower shrubs in planters. A white haired woman in long green gloves digging into black earth with a silver spade. No one on the sidewalks. A stop sign, a traffic light, two police cars in the parking lot of the Royal Farms. The next block: a smashed van in the parking lot of a service station, three rowhouses with For Sale signs.

Further on: the shell of a burned church — black skeleton of a steeple, black charred walls, yellow streamers of caution tape, white steps. Ben had the sensation that he was making the church exist by looking and he couldn't do it much longer and it was vibrating slightly and about to dissolve. He thought, I need a drink. It's just the day I'm having. I should just stop and have some food and maybe a drink and clear my head.

He took a right into another neighborhood, these rowhouses more ramshackle, with peeling paint, little front yards more of dirt than grass. A rat-like dog peering out through a low chainlink fence. Two teenagers (who should be in school, Ben saw) one carrying a skateboard, the other unpeeling a lollipop. A maybe four-year old girl, younger than his daughter, with wild pale curls, alone in her little yard, squatting down to plop a handful of dirt on top of a plastic pretend lawnmower, an old woman in a shapeless dress-that-looked-like-a-nightgown sitting in a lawn chair on the porch, watching her. A roofing company van with a thick Christian fish painted on the side. A giant PVC pipe yard sculpture of a bird in flight. A closed bakery, a drugstore with a Christmas tree in the window, a stone church. He took a left at the next light: a street of shops, a banner overhead across the street announcing a road race. Ben found a spot and parked and got out. There, a meter was blinking a red "EXPIRED," but Ben thought "Fuck it," and slammed his door and did not lock his car and did not pay.

Just ahead, a dark store, with swirly-patterned pottery among the shadows of the front window display. Next door was a bar called Gracie's, a plastic Bud Light banner draped above the window — half price drafts during Orioles games. The door swung open as he approached—a pale woman in a too-big white T-shirt walked right out into the street and across without looking. Ben could see in: a long bar, a TV high in the corner showing sports highlights, a grimacing young woman leaning into a video solitare machine, a thick man in a blue work-jumpsuit smoking a tipped cigar. Ben thought, "my father didn't smoke." He did not go in.

Further along, a locally-famous restaurant called Raccoon Brothers where they'd been to brunch a few times with friends, before the baby. The walls were tableaus of stuffed animals. A menu of items like grass-fed-Bison Burgers and chick-pea-battered onion rings that seemed too expensive for what it was, but Ben was very hungry. And there was a bar in back, he remembered. When he got closer he could see a group of vividly-flanneled art student types at the big table in the window. At a booth, a couple with a baby in a carrier, the baby sleeping. He walked by.

A pawn shop, a Korean restaurant, a comic book store.

At a cross street, a fire truck screamed by, lights whirling. Ben stopped by a lamppost to wait, to watch it go, to listen to the sound sink back into the city. And when the siren was gone the city was not quiet. His heart was racing. He had nowhere to go.

Just ahead, a few steps along the sloping-down cross street, a sign in curly bright yellow hand-painted letters: Always Never Records. A door propped open by what looked like a chunk of curb. Some kind of music, some kind of pulse, was coming from the open door. He went in.

The store was a very small, basement room. It had a concrete floor and smelled like his basement: damp concrete and sawdust, but also, faintly, the sweet grassy smell of good pot, something he hadn't smelled for years. The ceiling had been papered over with psychedelic-colored posters for rock shows thirty and forty years ago and the walls were woodpaneling probably left over from whatever the space had been before. Strings of jewel-bright Christmas lights were tacked up in jagged patterns on the walls, as if covering cracks. The store was crammed full with tables, nailed together plywood and 2-by-4s., and the tables were covered with crates and bins full of records.

Over the tables dangled wooden signs with curly bright yellow hand-painted letters: Indie. Dubstep. Bizarre. And, directly in front of him, Jazz. On the cover of the first record in the first bin there was a photograph of a pile of frogs squirming out of the bell of a saxophone. The only other customer in the store was a black-T-shirted young man with silver headphones around his neck, his back to the door, sorting through Soul.

Music — a watery chugging sound, laced through with strings of piano and a woman singing, her voice so distorted as to be unintelligible — was coming from speakers mounted on the wall in the back of the store. Between the speakers was the cash register, set up on a sort of raised platform. Behind the cash register were two people, a shaggy-haired young man seated, leaning back against the table, dark thick five-pointed stars on his forearms, partially blocked from Ben's view by an open silver laptop — the same laptop Mary Ann had. The young man was talking up to a young woman who was standing against the wall. She had a round face and pale blue eyes, dyed fire-red hair held back with a red headband. She was wearing a shapeless gray sweatshirt, hands stuffed into it as if she was cold.

I know her, thought Ben in the same instant as he saw how ridiculous the thought was. It was impossible. His daughter was closer to her age than he was. He was still watching her when she glanced over, said "Can I help you find something?" in a surprisingly scratchy voice, just loud enough to be heard over the music. It took Ben a few seconds to process that she was talking to him. He was in this store. It was impossible. He managed to shake his head, swallow. He felt a desperate urge to turn and walk out of the store so he made himself take a few steps further in and put his hands on the crate that held the record with the frogs coming out of the saxophone. When he glanced over again the red haired young woman had returned to listening to the shaggy-haired young man. He glanced behind him out the open door and saw that the daylight had thickened—either there were clouds moving over the sun or the afternoon was further along than he'd thought. Across the street, a white-blossomed pear tree shivered like a ghost and then the strange music cut out. The shaggy-haired young man had stood, and was lifting the shiny black record up from a turntable.

Ben heard in the empty space the music had left the traffic outside, the blood in his brain, and he looked at the photograph of the frogs in the saxophone and let his eyes unfocus and he thought to himself "I will let myself feel this now." And then he closed his eyes and made himself see the face of his wife and the face of his daughter. And he saw the face of his father, of his father's corpse—stiff and gray and unpeaceful forever. And he saw the face of his wife when she was young and drunk, beautiful, and listening to him for the first time in that dark dorm room. And he saw the body of his daughter there, stretched out in the muddy sand beneath the swing set, just at the moment she understood she was hurt, the moment before she started to scream. He had not been there. He had not saved her and could not save her. He loved her. He was a child; he was breathing in his last breath.

ACKNOWLEDGEMENTS

The author would like to thank the editors of the magazines where the following first appeared:

"The Dogs of Baltimore": *Avery*
"Dark Molly": *The Collagist*
"I Won the Bronze Medal": *Annalemma*
"John's Story": *Lunch Hour Stories*
"Henry": *Redivider*
"The Customer": *PANK*
"Hush": *South Carolina Review*
"The Wildflowers of Baltimore": *Epoch*

CPSIA information can be obtained at www.ICGtesting.com
Printed in the USA
BVOW011140151112

305657BV00002B/2/P